W9-AMB-561

## "Jake, it's our song!"

His brows shot up in a question. "I didn't know we had a song."

Hands on her hips, she shook her head at his cluelessness. "As chair of the prom committee, I selected the song for the king-and-queen dance. I knew we had received the most votes." A sad smile formed. "I picked it for us."

His forehead wrinkled. "You danced it with Tommy."

"'Cause *you* never showed up." She pointed the spatula at him. "*You* had the most votes. *You* were voted king. Because you weren't there I had to dance with Tommy."

She felt the warmth of his presence as he moved closer to her. He stopped two steps away from where she stood.

"We could dance it now."

**Books by Jolene Navarro**

Love Inspired

*Lone Star Holiday*
*Lone Star Hero*

### *JOLENE NAVARRO*

Jolene's life, much like her stories, is filled with faith, family, football, art, laughter, dirty dishes and all of life's wonderful messiness. She knows that, as much as the world changes, people stay the same. Good and evil. Vow-keepers and heartbreakers. Jolene married a vow-keeper who showed her that holding hands and dancing in the rain never gets old. When she's not teaching art to energetic middle-schoolers or hanging out with her four kids, she loves creating stories of love and faith in her much-loved Texas.

# Lone Star Hero

## Jolene Navarro

HARLEQUIN® LOVE INSPIRED®

If you purchased this book without a cover you should be aware that this book is stolen property. It was reported as "unsold and destroyed" to the publisher, and neither the author nor the publisher has received any payment for this "stripped book."

Recycling programs
for this product may
not exist in your area.

™ LOVE INSPIRED BOOKS

ISBN-13: 978-0-373-81785-6

LONE STAR HERO

Copyright © 2014 by Jolene Navarro

All rights reserved. Except for use in any review, the reproduction or utilization of this work in whole or in part in any form by any electronic, mechanical or other means, now known or hereinafter invented, including xerography, photocopying and recording, or in any information storage or retrieval system, is forbidden without the written permission of the editorial office, Love Inspired Books, 233 Broadway, New York, NY 10279 U.S.A.

This is a work of fiction. Names, characters, places and incidents are either the product of the author's imagination or are used fictitiously, and any resemblance to actual persons, living or dead, business establishments, events or locales is entirely coincidental.

This edition published by arrangement with Love Inspired Books.

® and TM are trademarks of Love Inspired Books, used under license. Trademarks indicated with ® are registered in the United States Patent and Trademark Office, the Canadian Intellectual Property Office and in other countries.

www.Harlequin.com

Printed in U.S.A.

You have journeyed up a steep, rugged path
in recent days. The way ahead is shrouded in
uncertainty. Look neither behind you nor before you.
Instead, focus your attention on Me, your constant
Companion. Trust that I will equip you fully
for whatever awaits you on your journey.
—*Psalms* 143:8

To my sisters Tracye Ward and Amanda Warren—
you have become amazing women and great
mothers. I know our parents would be proud.
Always to Fred Navarro, husband extraordinaire.

## Acknowledgments

There are so many people that made my dream
of being a writer become reality.

First to the gifted writers at San Antonio Romance
Authors for sharing their time and talents,
especially Linda Carroll-Bradd, who taught me
what POV meant and how to use it.

Joni, Marilyn, Sasha and Storm,
thank you for listening and reading.

To Jodi Thomas and Alexandra Sokolof,
two of the most talented and giving people I know.

To the best agent ever, Pam Hopkins.

To the remarkable Emily Rodmell, thank you for
giving me the opportunity to share Clear Water,
Texas, with the world. My stories are better
because of your insight and knowledge.

# *Chapter One*

The blue and red lights flashed. Polished cowboy boots stepped out of the looming SUV. Each step stirred pale dust into the dry air. She didn't need to look at his face to know who had pulled her over. Ever since her return to Clear Water, Texas, she had done her best to avoid this state trooper.

Jake Torres made it too easy to doubt her resolve to be independent. After a disastrous marriage with one hometown boy, she couldn't contemplate a relationship with another, even if he had been her best friend once upon a time.

Now her ex-friend was going to give her a ticket on Valentine's Day. Great. Another memento to add to this wonderful day.

Turning away from the rearview mirror, she glanced at the box of pink penguin cupcakes. They had taken her twice as long to decorate as she'd planned.

"Mom! We're going to be late!" Ashley, her seven-year-old daughter, cried from the backseat.

She closed her eyes for a moment to control the burning acid in her stomach.

More money gone. She didn't even have enough to buy her daughter the lollipop Valentine cards she wanted. With a quick check in the mirror, she noticed Ashley going through the handmade cards. A weak smile eased some of the tension as she thought of the fun they'd had while cutting and gluing scrap pieces of construction paper. Even Seth, her preteen son, had made a couple of glittery masterpieces.

An unwanted memory surfaced. The sparkly red heart she had created as an eleven-year-old. She could see Jake's fingers take the Valentine card made just for him. She'd held her breath watching him read the question she had so carefully printed. Looking up at her, he had smiled and laughed at her. "Vickie, you're crazy."

"Vickie?" A baritone voice of the grown version of her childhood crush brought her back to the present. He now stood in his state trooper uniform and looked at her as if he still doubted her sanity.

"Officer Torres." She replied in her most professional voice.

He leaned in a bit and looked past her. "Hi, Ashley. You're looking pretty today."

"Thank you. We're going to the horse club's Valentine's party."

He smiled and nodded before looking back at her. Well, she assumed he looked at her. With the dark aviators, all she saw was her own reflection. Not pretty.

"License and insurance?"

She handed him the documents. He always looked so good in cowboy hats. She made sure not to gaze at him. Instead, she focused on the empty country road stretched out in front of her. The outline of the hills surrounding them hid any sign of civilization.

A silver truck sped by and honked. Vickie scooted farther down in her seat and looked to her right. The Black Angus heifers went on with their eating. Her father's cattle couldn't care less about her problems.

"How is Seth doing?" Jake pulled her attention back to him.

Her knuckles went white around her worn and cracked steering wheel. Just two months ago, her son snuck out, making plans to run away and ended up in the shallow river in the dark. Her heart still stopped whenever she thought how close she came to losing her son. The image of his still form loaded into the ambulance burned forever in her mind.

"Last week the doctor released him for all regular activities. He's a hundred percent recovered, physically anyway." She took a breath and looked up. "Thank you for being there, for searching for him and helping me hold it together." It had been the worst night of her life, and Jake had stayed by her side until they found Seth. He drove her to the ambulance and helped her stay calm when it felt as if she was going to fall to pieces.

He paused and brought his face back to her. "I'm glad I was there. Vickie, you know if you ever need anything you can call me."

Yeah, that was Jake, everyone's hero. Giving her a speeding ticket, probably for her own good. "You wouldn't consider just giving me a warning, would you?" She tried to smile, but visions of her measly savings dwindling even further made it difficult.

"The sun's almost down. It's hard to see deer, and in your small car that can be dangerous. Just the other day..." His voice dropped off as he looked back to his new handheld scanner. "Um...Vickie?"

That didn't sound good. "Yes?"

"Are you aware you have a warrant out for your arrest?"

"What?" Her voice squeaked as it caught in her throat. "Oh, no! I had a ticket somewhere in East Texas. I didn't...oh, then Tommy and Seth..." She covered her face with her cold, clammy hands. *You will not cry, Victoria Maria Lawson. You will not cry.*

"Mommy?"

"Vickie, take a breath. It's okay. You have a way to pay it, right? You can ask your father." He took the dark shades off. "As soon as you pay it in full they'll remove the warrant."

"I'm not asking Daddy. I just forgot about it." Did she have enough in her savings? Was she ever going to get to the point where she put more in than she withdrew? She looked in the rearview mirror. Ashley's big eyes were even wider. "It's okay, sweetheart." She glanced up at Jake. "I have Ash…"

"Vickie. I don't want to arrest you, but you have to pay it. Call your dad. He'll help you."

"I have the money. I'm not asking Daddy to save me. I completely forgot… How could I…?" She closed her eyes and took a deep breath. How did she let this happen? With Seth's near-death excursion and Tommy getting remarried she just…

"Mommy, are we still going to the horse club meeting?"

Oh, Ashley. "I don…"

"Vickie, take her to the party." He lowered his chin and stared at her a moment before speaking again. "I'll follow. Ashley can go into the exhibit hall and you can take care of the ticket over the phone."

His thoughts were hidden behind the depth of his dark eyes. The intense gaze made her want to hide.

"Take it slow. Being late is not the worst thing that can happen." He glanced down. "You need new tires. These are bald, and your inspection sticker needs to be renewed." He took a step back.

She managed to nod. "Thank you. I can pay it. I just forgot." He didn't get it. She grew up relying on her parents then Tommy. She refused to ask them for help. She had to do this on her own.

She turned the key. Click... Click. *No!* She tried again. Nothing. *Come on. Please start.*

One more try. The engine started. *Yes!* So much for a grand exit. It didn't purr, not like the Mercedes she drove just two years ago. She reminded herself to be grateful for a car she bought with her own money. Pulling back onto the country road, she headed to the arena on the edge of town.

Back in the SUV, Jake turned off the flashing light. With a heavy sigh, he started the engine.

He spent years ignored by Vickie. *He should be used to it by now.* Nevertheless, seeing her so battered by life hurt him in a way he suspected he'd never get over.

After checking the empty road for traffic, he pulled out to follow her. He'd pay the ticket himself if it would keep him from having to arrest her. He imagined she'd never forgive him for putting her in jail in front of her daughter.

Vickie would never forgive him for helping her, either. Describing her as stubborn was like calling the Texas sun in August a little warm.

Just a couple of months ago her son had been airlifted to San Antonio after almost drowning. He thought they had connected that night and she would be more open to reviving their old friendship.

Going by the Mercantile where she worked, he

tried talking to her, but she managed to be in the back of the store whenever he stopped by.

Vickie made it clear that he had no place in her life.

He finally got to see her face-to-face, only to have to threaten to arrest her. Not the impression he wanted to make.

Easing into the parking spot next to Vickie's small vehicle, Jake put the Explorer in park in front of the sixty-year-old county building. The windows of the wood exhibit hall shimmered with pink and red metallic ribbons.

A couple of faces appeared through the streamers followed quickly by three girls rushing outside. "Ashley! Where have you been? You volunteered to decorate."

The oldest one, Rachel Levi, the pastor's daughter, stopped at the edge of the concrete slab and looked at Vickie instead of the younger girls. "Mrs. Lawson, is Seth with you?"

"No, sweetheart, he's with his grandfather." Vickie reached over and pulled the cupcakes out.

Ashley stood with her box of cards. "He's grounded. But he made a card for you."

"Really?" A smile lit up her face. The preteen turned to Vickie. "He's still grounded because we snuck out?"

"No, Rachel, he has a whole new set of reasons." Her lips drawn, the girl looked uncomfortable.

She had been with Seth the night he ran away and had pulled his unconscious body out of the river.

"Is your father here tonight?" Vickie asked.

Rachel nodded. "Daddy still doesn't allow me anywhere without him."

Jake looked at his watch. If Vickie was going to get her fines paid today, she needed to make those calls before the office closed.

He moved forward to take the cupcakes from her. "Come on, girls, let's get these inside. Ms. Lawson has some calls to make before the party starts."

Ashley and Celeste, Rachel's little sister, skipped to his side, holding hands. "Celeste, my mom made penguin cupcakes," Ashley said.

Rachel went in, shoulders slumped, but the other girls hopped around him.

"Oh, Ashley, these are the cutest cupcakes ever." Mia De La Cruz, one of Ashley's friends, held the door open for them.

At the far end of the room, women were setting the tables with food and drinks. He knew everyone. To his left Pastor John and Adrian De La Cruz kicked balloons out of their way as they walked toward him.

Adrian, a carpenter and roper Jake hung out with, slapped him on the back. "So you giving Ms. Lawson and her cupcakes a police escort?"

He smiled. "Looks that way, doesn't it? So where do these guys go?"

"I'll take them, Officer Torres." Rachel took the box from him and headed across the open floor.

Tables covered in more pink and red lined the walls. They left the center open for games and dancing. He spent many nights in his youth at the 4-H meetings and parties with Adrian and Vickie. "So now you're one of the 4-H parents?"

Adrian laughed. "That's me, dad of the Valentine's party. Happens a lot faster than you realize. Are you staying to help?"

"No, I just followed Vickie. I'm heading out, still on duty."

"Daddy!" Mia, Adrian's ten-year-old daughter, ran toward them. "Ms. Ortega is looking for the oranges and Hula-Hoops. Did you bring them in?"

"Yeah, I've got 'em." With another slap on Jake's back, Adrian followed his daughter to the group of mothers.

John gave him a quick goodbye and headed to his daughters.

Jake used to wonder what it would be like to have his own family. One part of him loved the thought of being the dad that helped at the 4-H events and rodeos, watching his own kids participate and compete. The other part knew he had no business being anyone's father or husband. The knowledge didn't seem to stop him from dreaming, though.

Vickie peeked around the door, scanning the area until she spotted him. She waved him over then disappeared outside.

For some insane reason, he smiled as he followed her through the door. Tomorrow she'd go back to ignoring him, but for now he had her full attention.

# *Chapter Two*

Vickie stood at her backyard fire pit alone, watching the dancing flames, the day finally over. She'd paid her ticket and left the party as soon as she could. Tomorrow would have been her thirteenth wedding anniversary. With the ugly emotions surfacing, it was a good thing Ashley went home with Mia, and Seth had stayed the night at her parents' house.

She had not had a second to herself in two months and tonight she needed some alone time. A fitting end to her worst Valentine's Day ever.

Well, maybe not the worst. Three years ago today, she found out her husband had been involved with his campaign manager, a woman she trusted. A woman that had sat at her dinner table and played with her kids. An anniversary gift she'd never forget.

She had worked so hard at being the good wife

to a man that didn't care about being a good husband or father. It was all about image for Tommy.

Dousing the fire pit with diesel, Vickie watched the flames dance high into the Texas night sky. Hands on her hips, she looked up, following the tongues of orange as they curled and danced toward the stars.

For a moment, she focused on the silhouetted hills surrounding her father's ranch. She grew up counting the trees along the riverbank. Their smell always gave her comfort, but not tonight.

Tonight she needed to do something to purge the remaining traces of bitterness and feeling of helplessness. Maybe a good cry. She snorted. Her mother would disapprove.

*Crying didn't solve anything, just made a person look weak.* Opening the elaborate cover of her wedding album, she looked at the engagement picture. That girl looked like a stranger to her now. She was made up in the image of her mother.

Tommy smiled at the camera, one arm wrapped around her waist. Her hand flat against his shirt, showing off the large diamond. She tossed the grinning groom into the blaze and stared as his face distorted before vanishing into ashes.

She couldn't think of one single day in the last two years she had even missed Tommy and his hypercritical demands. Finding out about the other woman was her breaking point. He blamed her, telling her he couldn't love her.

Being a wife and mother was all she ever wanted. She didn't seem to be winning in that department, either. She rolled her head back and closed her tired eyes.

A grown woman with an eleven-year-old son and seven-year-old daughter to raise and not a marketable skill in sight.

Her mother lectured her for the past twelve years about being the good wife, even after the divorce. *People in her family did not get divorced.*

Against all evidence, Elizabeth Lawson hung on to the dream that Tommy would come back and beg her forgiveness, becoming the model family man. Vickie knew it was beyond over. She failed at marriage and had messed up the perfect family history. Her mother would have to find a way to deal.

The one thing she would not be, could not be, was a failure at being a mom. Her kids needed her more than ever since Tommy's disappearing act.

She tore out another photo, her mother fussing over the intricate pile of hair the hairdresser had created around the bridal veil. Miles of perfectly preserved white lace and tiny beaded pearls surrounded Vickie along with all her mother's plans and expectations.

Seth needed her to be strong. She knew the divorce and his father's abandonment hurt him beyond words.

Flipping the heavy page, she ripped out another

photo. Into the fire the kiss went. Running down the steps of the church...gone.

The three-foot wedding cake...history.

The breeze blew smoke into her face. Vickie's chest and throat started to burn as tears finally escaped, one after another. Her eyesight blurred as she watched each picture vanish in the multicolored inferno.

Headlights made their way down the long drive. She gritted her teeth. Why couldn't her mother just leave her alone in her misery? Using the bottom of her oversize T-shirt, Vickie wiped her face.

The car door opened and closed.

"Vickie?" A strong, masculine voice surprised her. She hung her head. Much worse than her mother, the ex-best friend that almost arrested her today. Officer Jake Torres.

"I could see the flames from the highway. You know the county is in the middle of a burn ban." He walked straight toward her.

She pretended not to notice his wide shoulders or powerful legs. He was a walking cliché of a Texas Ranger. "Officer Torres, I would think you had better things to do than bother women—" A leftover sob escaped her chest. She swallowed it back down "—on their own property. Is this an arrestable offense also?"

He sat on his heels, hunched next to her as he picked up a picture that had fallen in the dirt. "Wedding pictures?"

She stared at the fire, hoping he would leave. She didn't want to share her humiliation with anyone, especially her childhood crush. Every girl at school had giggled whenever Jake walked by. He had been her best friend but completely out of reach.

He thrust his chin to the box at her feet. "In honor of your anniversary?"

She turned to him in shock. "You remembered my wedding date? Tommy never did." She should look away. *Please, just go away before I start to think I could rely on you.* "You weren't even there."

This time he broke eye contact first. "Yeah, I... um... I had to be somewhere else."

*Why didn't you take me with you?* "You had to run off and save the world."

He reached out and touched her arm. His dark hand stood in contrast to her pale skin.

"Vickie, are you all right? Has Tommy done something?" She jerked her arm back. *Don't let him think you need a friend, Victoria Maria.* She turned her face away from him and focused on the fire. "I'm fine. This is not about Tommy. He's in Florida planning his new future, and I'm here with the kids. That's all I need." *Please leave before I do something stupid like cry in front of you.*

He pulled his hand back and stood. "You're a good mother. Listen, I know you've had a couple of rough years, but you have people that are here for you if you need anything."

The problem with that was she needed to learn

to take care of herself. Swallowing the lump in her throat, she focused on the popping of the fire. Maybe if she ignored him, he'd go away.

Looking around, he spotted the green water hose, neatly curled up like a snake. With a turn of the old knob, he had the water running full blast. Stretching the hose from the old barn to the pit, he started smothering the flames. Jake scanned the area for any wayward embers.

Vickie burst from her chair almost eye to eye with him, even barefoot. He always liked her height. He frowned. Was that the problem? His mother was always trying to match him up with short women.

"Hey! That's my fire. Just because you wear a uniform now doesn't mean you…"

"Victoria, it's so dry, the smallest spark could turn your father's ranch into an inferno."

Standing, she crossed her arms over her chest and glowered at him.

He smiled.

The hostility in her glare was so much better than the defeated look he saw earlier.

With a deep sigh, she looked away and ran her fingers through her dark blond mane. "I'm sorry."

Tonight her hair hung loose, looking wild as the flames reflected off the long strands. He loved it down. Most of the time, she kept it styled and starched. He had to lean in a bit to hear what she muttered.

"I don't know why I say the things I do. It just pops in my head and out of my mouth." She turned her face back to him. Her eyelashes glistened with moisture. "I'm so tired of fighting. Seth and I had another argument earlier today."

Jake concentrated on putting out the flames. He could control this fire for her. He had no idea how to help her with the rest of her life. "Don't be so hard on yourself. Talk to him, explain what's going on. Believe me, sons are very forgiving of their mothers."

He shoveled some dirt from the nearby mound into the pit. The last of the flames died out, separating them with a column of thick smoke.

She flopped back down in the camping chair. "I'm sure he'd be much happier without me as his mother." She closed her eyes. "I can't blame him. I don't want to be around me, either."

"Seth loves you. He's just angry and confused right now. Give him some time." He coiled the hose. Standing a good ten feet away, he could still see her shivering as she huddled into a ball.

With the fire out, all the heat vanished, leaving the cold breeze and smoke between them.

He didn't want to leave, but he had to get going.

A few steps and he was next to her. He slipped off his jacket and laid it over her thin T-shirt. Sitting on his heels next to the camouflaged chair, his hand resting on the canvas arm, as close to her as possible without touching, he said, "Listen, Vickie,

I know it's been a tough couple of years, but life will get better."

"Thanks." Her tight-lipped answer gave him the first clue that their friendly discussion had ended about as fast as it had started.

He stood. "Call me if you need anything." Like the hardheaded idiot he was, he waited. After a few extensive minutes loaded with nothing but his own breathing, Jake stepped back. "Good night, Victoria." Another pause, just to make sure she had nothing else to say.

With a locked jaw, he walked to his patrol car. He forced himself to look straight ahead, no turning back, not one glance over his shoulder. No, she had made it clear over the years she didn't need him. So why did he think tonight would be any different?

Vickie watched as each step took Jake farther away from her. She bit her lip as her fingernails cut into her palms. The urge to call him ripped at her throat. He slipped into his black SUV and reversed out of her drive. A new type of sadness wrapped itself around her heart. She hadn't felt so alone with him next to her.

Thick smoke rose from the fire pit. She wanted to throw her whole album into the now-soggy, mud-filled hole, but it was a part of her children's history. A part of her history—the good, bad and ugly.

Instead of dwelling on old hurts, she knew her time would be better spent focusing on the good and reading her Bible. Two months ago, holding her unconscious son's cold hand, she prayed for God's forgiveness, wise words and a new heart.

She had released the bitterness and anger; now she needed to put that new life into action. So many people deserved apologies from her. Where did she start?

Vickie walked back into her little single-wide trailer. For a second the thin walls of the narrow trailer closed in on her. It had been their temporary home for almost two years now. A stark difference to the three-thousand-square-foot home they had in San Antonio.

That life was gone, along with the money and the delusion of a happy ever after.

Snuggling deeper into the sturdy jacket, Jake's warmth and scent surrounded her —outdoors and leather.

On the faux-wood coffee table sat the Bible her father handed her when she signed the divorce papers. All he ever said about the whole mess was, "Stay focused on your faith. The Lord has you."

Why didn't God give her a man of faith like her dad?

She let the pages fall open. She had marked Jeremiah 16:19 on the night she sat in the waiting room when her son had almost died. "'The Lord is my strength and my fortress, my refuge in times of trouble.'" Her soft words helped fill the emptiness.

Jake had given her that verse on the way to the ambulance. God would be her refuge. She moved to the last door in the tiny hall. Her son was hurting. She grew up with two sisters and had no idea how to deal with an eleven-year-old boy that wanted his father.

He'd gotten so angry when she told him he wouldn't be going to Tommy's wedding. He blamed her for everything, the divorce, his father's leaving, his trouble with Rachel.

She protected the children from the worst of the betrayals, but she was losing her son.

Tommy wanted to focus on his new bride without the kids around. Her fingers gripped the edges of the cherished Bible. Of course, he made her tell the kids.

Leaning her forehead against the handmade warning sign taped to his door, she softly prayed. "God, please lift me up to be the kind of mother my children need. Cover Seth and Ashley in your love."

The trailer filled with heavy silence. She laid a hand against the plastic trim to support her now-weak legs. "I love Seth and Ashley so much. Thank you for the gift of being their mother." She waited for a heartbeat…two… "Help me use the right words with them to heal any hurts."

The phone rang. Instead of answering, she moved to the freezer and pulled out the vanilla ice cream.

"Victoria Maria, it's your mother." Her mother's sweet Texas drawl was leftover from her Dallas debutante days.

She was getting better at ignoring it.

"I need to talk to you about Seth." Her mother continued. "I know you're in that trailer."

Vickie could hear the disgust in her mother's tone. Each time she came to the house, her mother looked around the room as if she had found a roach running across the toes of her high-heeled shoes. Vickie closed her eyes and waited.

"Victoria Maria Miller, pick up."

Elizabeth Marie Lawson never screamed, shouted or yelled, but she had a voice of steel and she expected to be obeyed.

With a heavy sigh, Vickie picked up the landline with one hand and used the other to fill her mouth with ice cream.

She knew it was a petty form of rebellion, but it felt good to answer while still chewing.

"Mother, I'm not his wife anymore...." She made sure to swallow loudly, "and I'm back to Lawson."

"Are you eating while talking to me?"

Vickie put the spoon in the sink. "Sorry, Mama."

"Sweetheart, I'm not sure if going back to Lawson is the best thing for the children. They should have the same last name as their mother. I think it is upsetting Seth."

"Mom, everything upsets Seth." She wanted to curl up in bed, pull the blankets over her head and not listen to her mother's lecture. "Mom, it's been a really long day. Is Seth okay? Do I need to pick him up?"

"No, no. I think it's good for him to be around his grandfather. He needs a strong man of faith in his life. We were praying for his father, and Seth said you won't talk to Tommy when he calls."

"Mom, Tommy is getting married in less than a week." She hung her head and rubbed her forehead. "Please don't encourage Seth in the idea his father is coming back."

On the counter, her cell phone started vibrating.

"Victoria, he should…"

"Sorry to cut you off, Mom, but Lorrie Ann is on my cell. I should take it."

"Oh, I hope everything is okay. Why would she be calling you?"

"I don't know. Love you, bye." With a flip of her thumb, she received the call while hanging up on her mother.

"Lorrie Ann?" She couldn't image why Pastor Levi's fiancée was calling her. Slight nausea rolled her stomach. In Vickie's darkest moments, she delivered some of her ugliest words straight at Lorrie Ann. Bitterness, jealously and anger filled her thoughts just two months ago. Embarrassment made her want to disconnect the call.

"Hi, Vickie. Sorry to be calling late, but I was organizing my weekly schedule. I have a couple of ideas I would love to talk to you about. Could

I come over Friday night? It's about the wedding and the youth program." She laughed. "Right now it seems everything in my life is about the wedding. Would seven o'clock work for you? Oh, sorry. I'm being a little pushy. Between Aunt Maggie, my mom and Yolanda, not to mention every woman in the church who sees John as their adopted son, I'm going a little crazy."

"Um…no problem. You can come over." Vickie had no idea what to say. "You're always welcome here, and I owe you so much. Whatever you need, sign me up."

"Be careful what you say. I will hold you to it. See you Friday, and please have an open mind. Bye."

Vickie ended the call and sat there on the tall stool, looking at the phone. Twelve years ago, she had been jealous of Lorrie Ann and Jake's friendship, and pulled the mean-girl trick. She started lies about the girl she considered a rival. Hurtful, horrible lies and when they grew, she remained silent. She didn't do any better when Lorrie Ann came back to town over three months ago. Her eyes started to burn.

Somehow she was the girl everyone hated, but they were too afraid to say anything to her. The idea of someone treating her children like that tore at her heart.

She took a deep breath. *Take the good in.* She

exhaled, pushing her lungs until they burned. *Forcing all the bad out. "God, thank You for this opportunity to make it right."*

# *Chapter Three*

Friday arrived too soon. Tonight Lorrie Ann Ortega would be in Vickie's trailer. She swallowed down the butterflies that fluttered up from her stomach. Maybe she should call her and meet somewhere in town. No, doing this in public might even be worse.

Vickie practiced her apology, but it never sounded right. Putting away the clean dishes in the cabinet, she checked the small living room to make sure it was as clean and neat as she could get it. Jake's sturdy jacket lay over the back of one of the ladder-backed chairs. Picking it up, she ran her hand over the brown fabric.

Maybe she should take it to him. Vickie imagined showing up at his house. Would he welcome her or ask her to leave?

Okay, now she was overanalyzing returning a jacket. As she hung the coat in the hall closet, she heard a vehicle pull up to her drive.

Checking her clock, she figured it was Adrian. He had volunteered to pick up Ashley and take her to the regular horse club meeting.

Her daughter stomped from the tiny hallway. "Mom, my boots hurt my feet."

She hunched down in front of Ashley and checked the toes of the red boots. She sighed. Sure enough, the little toes pushed against the rounded end of the boots. She did a quick calculation of her next paycheck versus bills to be paid. Well, there went the last bit of her savings. "Sweetheart, they're too small for you. You're going to have to wear your tennis shoes until we can get you some more."

"I can just curl my toes." She looked down, her hair covering her face. "See. It doesn't hurt."

"Oh, baby, you can't wear shoes too small. You're not riding tonight, so go get your tennis shoes."

As Ashley stomped back to her room, she heard a knock. Opening the door, she greeted Adrian. Vickie glanced over his shoulder where his truck idled.

Mia waved from the backseat of the black truck. A large horse trailer with two horses inside filled her driveway.

"Oh, no, I thought tonight was just a meeting. I'm sorry, Adrian. I could've asked my dad to take her and one of his horses." Ashley was going to be so upset.

Adrian smiled. "No worries. We single parents have to stick together." He winked at her.

Vickie glanced to the side, not sure how to respond. Did Adrian just wink at her? He was younger than she was by a couple of years. Not knowing what to say she just stood there in silence.

He pointed to the silver trailer. "I have Cinnamon. She's old but refuses to be left behind. Ashley can ride her. Jake offered to go over some basic horse safety guidelines with the kids, and we thought it would be fun if they all actually had a horse. Hands-on learning."

Ashley came to the door. "Hi, Mr. De La Cruz. Is Mia with you? Oh, you have horses." Bright eyes filled with worry looked up at Vickie. "Mommy, you said we weren't riding. I need my boots."

Vickie glanced at Adrian and gave him a weak smile. "It seems like overnight they got too small for her." She pulled Ashley against her side. "Sweetheart, it's okay."

He pointed to the horse trailer. "I'm sure we have some of Mia's old boots in the dressing room." He gave them a lopsided grin. "I'm not the best at cleaning out the old stuff, and Mia seems to grow faster than a newborn colt, too. We probably have some you can borrow."

Vickie hated charity of any kind. "Are you sure? It would just be for tonight."

"Hey, you would be helping me out." He looked at Ashley. "You ready?"

With a nod, she hugged Vickie. "Love you, Mommy."

"Be careful." Vickie's words landed on departing backs. As they climbed into the huge truck, a Jeep Cherokee approached the trailer. Vickie didn't recognize the SUV. Adrian honked as he drove past the Jeep.

Lorrie Ann got out of the vehicle and went to the backseat. A knot formed in Vickie's stomach. She had thrown some hateful words at Lorrie Ann over the years, first in high school then even worse a few months back when Lorrie Ann had returned to town.

As a grown woman, she had no excuse for such behavior. Jealousy created some ugly side effects. If she really wanted to be a better person, God was giving her a great opportunity to make it right and start on her list of apologies.

She would start right here with Lorrie Ann. Tomorrow she could move on to Jake then maybe find a way to ask for forgiveness from the whole town of Clear Water.

She started down the steps. "Hi, Lorrie Ann. What happened to your BMW?"

Lorrie Ann opened the back door and leaned in. "Traded it in for something more practical."

"Do you need any help?" Vickie asked.

Lorrie Ann came out from behind the door with a bag. "That would be great. Here's some samples of materials. Aunt Maggie and Rachel made the dinner for y'all. It's a casserole so you can put it in the fridge and use it anytime you need a quick meal. Celeste and I made the cookies." She went back into the Jeep for the aluminum trays. Turning to Vickie, she had a big grin on her face. "Rachel also made a card and note. She wanted to make sure Seth got those. She missed him at the party."

Oh, great, she'd hoped they had put an end to the budding romance between her son and Pastor John's daughter. "Is her father okay with it?"

"Oh, he'll be fine. The note is very sweet and innocent. I think they're friends more than anything else." Lorrie Ann shrugged.

Vickie had fallen in love with Jake Torres when she was just ten but had been too afraid of her mother to let anyone know. Looking back, she realized it had probably been that secret that made her so mean to any girl brave enough to talk with Jake. Lies and fear had a way of festering.

"Are you ready to talk wedding?"

Vickie nodded and led Lorrie Ann into her trailer. Placing the items on the kitchen counter, Vickie closed her eyes and took a deep breath. A minute to relax the knot in her gut and let the bad out. "Lorrie Ann, I can't thank you enough for all you have done for me and Seth. You really didn't have to do this."

"Oh, I have alternative motives. Consider it a peace offering and bribe all rolled up into one."

"A peace offering? For what? I'm the one that owes you an apology and a huge thank-you for saving my son's life."

"I'm so glad I was there and could help. How is Seth doing?"

"Dr. Adams released him for all activities." *Now, Vickie. Speak up now.* "Can I get you some tea or lemonade?"

Lorrie Ann sat on the bar stool. "Lemonade would be great. Vickie, I need to ask a huge favor from you."

Pulling two of the best glasses from the cabinet, surprise derailed Vickie's thoughts for a moment. "Umm… You need something from me? Okay, just tell me what it is and I'll do it."

Lorrie Ann laughed. "I haven't even asked you yet."

As she filled the glasses with ice, Vickie struggled with the right words. "I owe you. Not only for finding Seth and knowing CPR, which I could never repay, but also for all the hateful rumors I started and the names I called you." She still had her back to Lorrie Ann as she poured the lemonade.

On a deep breath, she turned and slid the full glass across the counter. She looked Lorrie Ann in the eyes. The stunning gray and green swirls were even more beautiful because of the sweet compassion Vickie found in them. "I know it's old history and way too late, but I need to apologize for all the nasty rumors I started in high school. I was so jealous of the friendship you had with Jake. I wanted to hurt you. It was wrong of me." There. She did it and the world still moved in the right direction. "You left town because of me. I'm so sorry."

Lorrie Ann reached across the old, stained linoleum and laid her hands over Vickie's, forcing them to be still. "Thank you. I had my own issues, too. John told me not long ago that the choices and mistakes of our past don't have to shape our future, but they can be used to help others." She sat back and took a drink of her lemonade. "The part I didn't understand was why you were jealous. Back then, Jake only had eyes for you. Everyone knew that."

Vickie looked at her glass before taking her own sip. For a moment, she allowed the sweet, sour taste to fill her senses. She glanced out the window to the barn. "I was so in love with him, but I feared my mother's disapproval even more." With a weak grin, she looked back at Lorrie Ann. "My mom had a plan for me and it did not include the maid's son." She started wiping the counter. "Complete coward would be a good description of me. I owe you even a larger apology for my behavior when you returned to town. I was a bitter shrew, and as a grown woman, there was no excuse for my actions. I don't have any adequate words to tell you how sorry I am. So yes, I vow, whatever you need from me is yours."

"Well, you might regret that promise." Lorrie Ann leaned in closer and smiled. "I want to hire you to make my bridesmaids' dresses and two mother-of-the-bride dresses. One for Aunt Maggie and one for my mother, along with dresses for Rachel and Celeste. I would also love to work with you to design my wedding dress. And if you survive that, John's house is in major need of drapes, curtains and throw pillows."

Vickie didn't know what to say. She couldn't get her mouth to move.

Lorrie Ann took another drink before patting Vickie's hand. "Are you okay?"

"I lied about you and tried to run you out of town and you want me to make the dresses for your wedding?"

"You've apologized and I'm tired of holding grudges. Anyway, one of the things I learned in L.A. was business above personal feelings. You, Vickie, are the most amazing and talented seamstress I have ever seen. I also wanted to talk to you about helping out with the youth program. John, Jake and Rhody have a strong program for the boys, but I was thinking about other activities we could offer, sewing maybe, or some sort of arts or crafts. What do you think?"

Truly humbled by Lorrie Ann's acceptance, Vickie bit back the urge to cry. "I would love to help at the church. And I'll give you a discount for the dresses."

"Don't you dare. I'll pay you half as a down payment on Monday. You're going to earn every penny just dealing with my family." Lorrie Ann stood. "Thank you so much for the lemonade. And the apology. I really appreciate it." She leaned in and wiggled her eyebrows. "We might be related some-day if Seth and Rachel turn into real sweethearts. Don't you tell John I said that. He would have a heart attack. I'll see you later, Vickie. Maybe Sunday we can talk to John about ideas for the youth program."

Vickie led her to the door and waved as she watched her disappear through the gate. God does work in mysterious ways. In a million years, she would have never dreamed she'd be making the dresses for Lorrie Ann's wedding. She also had money to buy Ashley the new boots she needed. Tomorrow she would take Jake's jacket to him. Would she find another friend in Jake or was it too late?

# Chapter Four

Putting her car in Park, Vickie looked at the surrounding area. Jake had bought a beautiful piece of land to build his home.

Reaching over to the passenger's seat, Vickie gripped the sturdy jacket in her hands and stared at his two-story cabin. With the last rays of sun slipping over the hills, the richness of the wood called to her, begging her to come closer. Why did she sit out here hiding in her car, unsure?

Because she let her mother's words re-create all the self-doubt she'd been fighting. No more. She had a new life, a new purpose and needed some old friends. She could be just friends with Jake. She could.

With determination, she stepped out of her car and moved up the gravel walkway to the deep wraparound porch. Her hand caressed the smooth railing as she climbed the wide steps. The huge glass door sparkled from the waning light.

"I can take the jacket."

The female voice from deep in the porch caused her to jump. Placing her hand flat against her racing heart, Vickie turned to face Maria Torres, Jake's mother.

"I didn't see you there." Vickie moved to the swing at the end of the porch.

"There's no reason for you to go inside." Maria closed her Bible and set it to the side. The slight Spanish accent softened her words. "I can make sure he gets it. Just lay it there in the rocking chair."

"I…would like to thank him for helping me the other night." Vickie looked back to the door. Maybe she had made a mistake. Trying to recapture some youthful fantasy that had never even been real wasn't a good idea.

Maria's eyebrows went up. "Yes, Jake is very good at helping people. I hear Seth has fully recovered. I've been praying for him." Maria folded her hands in her lap and gently swung, the chains creaking over the wood.

"Thank you for your prayers. I know they helped. The doctors said he was very fortunate."

"Our children are our most precious gifts from God. We must protect them. Right? As mothers we understand the big picture."

Vickie didn't like where this was going. "Right. But as they grow up, we have to allow them to make their own choices."

"True. Let me speak honest with you, Mrs.

Miller." She smoothed out her blouse, her accent thicker now. "You have hurt Jake in the past, a hurt that was not easy for him to get over. I lost him once because of you. You might care for him now, but we both know you are not what he needs. Please do not pull him back into your life."

Horrified that Maria blamed her for him leaving for the marines the day after graduation, Vickie looked down to the wood boards. She heard he had built this house with his own hands. Vickie laid the jacket on the empty rocker. "I'm no longer Miller. It's just Lawson now." She bit into her bottom lip and looked at the setting sun. "No disrespect, Mrs. Torres, but I was not the one who left without a word."

"If you truly want what is best for him, you will stay away from him."

"Mother!"

Jake's voice startled both women.

"I'm old enough to pick my own friends." Jake stood at the far edge of the house. The setting sun cast him in silhouette, a bridle in his hand.

How long had he been standing there?

Maria stood and headed for the door. Toting her Bible, she nodded to Vickie. "I'm going to make dinner." Without a backward glance, she marched to the cut-glass door. With her head up, she swung the door open and glided through it. The gentle but firm click reminded Vickie that she had no right to enter Jake's world.

Hanging the leather headset and braided reins on a hook, Jake made his way up the steps. "Sorry about that." He sent her one of his heart-stopping grins.

She could spend hours staring at his smile. Sighing, she pulled herself back to reality. She was lying to herself; she wanted more than friendship with Jake Torres, and that could not happen.

He moved to the swing his mother had just abandoned and patted the space next to him. "As you know, mothers can get protective, no matter what age their children are."

Shaking her head, Vickie edged toward the railing, putting more distance between them. "She has a point."

"Come on, sit and tell me how Seth's doing." He leaned back, stretching his arms across the back of the seat.

His offer tempted her. She gripped the railing, keeping herself away from him. "He's good, ready to get back to all his regular activities."

"There's a father-and-son flag-football game coming up at the church picnic in a couple of weeks. It's part of our mentoring program at the church. We've been practicing." He grinned. "More like an excuse to throw the ball around and have fun. I thought I could take Seth. If he's ready, would he like that?"

"Oh, he loves football. Well, he did, anyway. The last couple of times he played with the YMCA in

San Antonio were rough. Tommy had high expectations. He made Seth play quarterback." She looked down at her feet, and followed the patterns made by the grains of wood. "Well, you know how Tommy is on the field. No room for mistakes." She looked back at Jake. "He might not want to play anymore."

Jake grunted and looked to the hills, the sun almost gone. "Yeah, I know Tommy. Spent way too many years on the field with him. But there's more to football than quarterbacking." He looked back toward her, his dark eyes intense in the last rays of light. "If you don't mind, I'd love to take Seth and reintroduce him to the fun of football. It's flag, so not much hitting. Is that okay with you?"

"Yeah, thank you. It'll be good for him to be around other boys. He hasn't made many friends since we came back."

"You could use a friend, too. You and Ashley can join us. We could grab something to eat afterward."

For a moment, she imagined them all together, almost like a real family. Her gaze traveled the outline of his house. If she had made the right choice in high school, this warm home and special man could've been hers. But she hadn't. The reality of it hit her hard. As much as she would love to reconnect with Jake, she had to put her life back in order, starting with her kids.

Her kids were the best part of her life. The one thing she got right with Tommy.

Her baggage was too heavy to leave on Jake's

steps. Friendship with Jake sounded good, but now she knew she'd want more.

She made so many wrong choices and it was too late to change them. "Jake, your mother's right. I'm not what you need."

He leaned forward, elbows planted on his knees. "Why don't you and my mother let me decide what I need?"

His intense stare seared right to her heart. She couldn't handle that look right now. Vickie stepped back. "I've got to go. The kids are waiting for me at my parents' house. Bye, Jake." She ran to her car, clenching her teeth.

It took two tries for her car to start. She was not good at the dramatic exit. She pulled out of his drive and with one last glance into the rearview mirror, she saw Jake at the top of the steps, watching her. There wasn't enough light to see his expression.

She needed to focus on the road in front of her. Heading back to her small trailer, Vickie fought the urge to cry for the girl that had not been strong enough to be the woman Jake needed when they were in high school.

Jake paused in the archway leading to his kitchen. He watched his mother as she lifted the lid to stir the contents of the steaming pot. The rich aroma of the *carne guisada* encouraged him to forget what he wanted to say. No, he wouldn't let her cooking distract him. They needed to get some things straightened out.

"Sit, *mijo*, dinner's almost done."

So she wanted to pretend nothing had happened with Vickie. Not this time.

"Mother, I love you, but I'm a grown man. I don't need you to pick my friends." Standing at the sink to wash his hands, Jake looked over his backyard. The surrounding hills created a cocoon around the pasture. In the twilight, he could make out his pair of roping horses.

He had put together a life he loved. He just never found anyone to share it with, well, other than Vickie. His mind always went back to her. "You had no right to be rude to Vickie."

"She's not your friend. She made her choice and married Tommy Miller. And you do need help. You are almost thirty-one and not married. I should have grandchildren." She filled two plates with the mouth-watering sauce and meat and set them on the table. Hands in her lap she waited for Jake to join her before continuing. "I remember your pain after she went with that boy to the prom."

He tried not to roll his eyes. "That's old history. Vickie's divorced now. She was married to the wrong man. You should understand that better than anyone." He dug a fork into his dinner. "If I want to pursue a relationship with Vickie, that's my business." He looked at his mother, pointing the meat-loaded utensil at her. "Please be nice to her."

Across from him, she picked at her plate. "I just don't want to see you get hurt again. You need to move on, and I need grandchildren in my old age. Your sister has run off and shows no sign of settling down."

Jake grinned. "*Amá*, she didn't run away. She's studying to be a lawyer."

"Yes, well, she made it clear she has no desire to get married." She looked around the large kitchen that opened to a cozy family room. "It's my fault. Look at this beautiful home you made. You built this home for a family, but the only kids ever here are the youth groups from the church. You deserve a family of your own." She looked him straight in the eyes, lips firm. "I deserve grandchildren."

"I think you might have already said that a few hundred times." He used a warm corn tortilla to soak up the gravy on the beef tips. "There's a side to Vickie no one gets to see."

"Maybe you're blind to what everyone else knows about her. She is her mother's daughter."

His jaw flexed. "And I'm my father's son."

Maria gasped and reached for his hand. "No. Oh, *mijo,* don't ever say that!"

"Did you forget what I did?"

She stood, the chair toddling on back legs before settling down. "No! You will not speak of that. The fault was mine." She picked up her Bible. "You are not your father, you're not!"

Jake pushed away from the table and pulled his

mother into his arms, hugging her short frame against his chest. "I'm sorry, *amá*. I shouldn't have said anything." He closed his eyes and buried his guilt. "I just wanted you to know the Vickie I know. The summer we moved here, well, she helped me…I don't know, she helped me in ways I can't explain."

"I remember her as a sweet girl, I do, but you are from different worlds." Her head shook against his chest before stepping away. "I was their house-keeper. It would be easier if you turned your attention to someone more like us."

"Mother, we've already had this conversation." He sighed.

"Maybe you hang on to your love for her because she's safe?"

As the words sank in, he stared at his tiny mother. Safe, with no risk of being in a real relationship. Did he? Vickie had always kept him at a distance, no jealous rages to worry about.

His mother went to the sink and ran the wash-cloth under the water. "You're a good man, Jake." Keeping her eyes down, she started wiping the counter. "Juan always bullied—his sisters, me, even his dogs." Her lips tight, she neatly folded the dishrag and draped it over the pewter faucet. "But enough of that nonsense."

For a moment Jake's brain echoed her words. She never, ever mentioned his father by name. Never spoke of him.

"Here, take this." She slipped a blue piece of paper from her Bible and held it out until he automatically took the handwritten number. "This is Anjelica Ortega's cell phone number. Her mother gave it to me. We know you'll be perfect together. She needs an honorable man after losing her husband. Call her. She's waiting to hear from you. If nothing else, it's just a date, right? When was the last time you went out for fun?"

With a sigh, Jake took the number and slipped it into his wallet, hoping that simple action would put the discussion to rest for now.

His mother meant well. She truly believed he needed a wife and children to be happy. He had tried dating, and it never felt right.

He remembered Anjelica and Steve from school. They were younger and always together. No one had been surprised when they married a month after graduation and two months later, he went to boot camp. In less than a year, she was a war widow. That was years ago. He hadn't seen much of her in town.

He hadn't seen much of Vickie, either. She was always working at the Mercantile or hiding on the ranch. She had made the first step by coming to his home. But then she ran off, putting distance between them, *again*.

This time he would follow her. There was no reason to tell his one-track-minded mother his new plan.

He pushed his hair off his forehead and flexed his jaw. Right now, his brain needed a break from all this emotional turmoil. He didn't want to think about Anjelica and her young soldier *or* Vickie and the coward she had married.

He flopped down on the overstuffed leather sofa and wrapped his fingers around his remote. He just wanted to watch some football for the next few hours. Tomorrow he would map out a plan to get to know Vickie again. Seth needed guidance, too. He knew from firsthand experience that having a bad father was worse than not having one at all. The flag football game would be a good place to undo any damage Tommy might have caused to the boy's confidence.

# *Chapter Five*

Jake pulled his black Silverado to the front of Vickie's trailer. He grinned as he leaned over the steering wheel. Who would have thought Vickie Maria Lawson would choose to live in the old worker's house.

Two decades had passed since his mother had taken the job as the Lawsons' housekeeper. The rent-free trailer had been one of the benefits. Coming from a tiny, one-room house in the crowded border-town of Eagle Pass, this single-wide trailer felt huge. For the first time he'd had his own room, his own bed.

Stepping out of his truck, Jake heard music blaring from the narrow trailer. The tune sounded like something from their high school days.

On the first step, the worn wood gave and dangerously shifted under his weight. That needed to be fixed. He jotted the note in his mind.

He wondered why she moved in here instead of

her parents' house. The big house, as they called it growing up, could easily fit five families.

He remembered his first trip to the *big house*. Looking over from his old home, he had once thought the trailer a mansion. A grin followed a chuckle. The Lawson home had awed him with the massive rooms, winding staircases and endless hallways, making him feel he had fallen down the rabbit's hole into Alice's Wonderland.

He remembered the moment the oldest daughter, Miss Victoria Lawson, entered the grand room. Struck dumb would be an understatement.

Until the next week, anyway, when he found her in the old barn behind his trailer, sitting in the dirt, wearing a ratty T-shirt. She was feeding three abandoned lambs, laughing as they climbed over her, fighting for the bottle she held.

He smiled. Her laughter from that day would be forever branded in his memory.

The other night he had tried to explain to his mother how Vickie had helped him. She had done so much for him that summer. She had saved him from falling into a deep, dark hole of despair.

She now lived in his old house. If he hadn't believed before, he absolutely knew God enjoyed a sweet bit of irony.

With a deep inhale, he moved forward. They were no longer kids hiding from their mothers or teenagers trying to figure out life. Maybe *this* time they could get it right.

The music covered his knock. Jake could smell freshly baked cookies as he eased open her unlocked door. He would need to talk to her about that safety issue, mental note number two.

Pausing in the door frame, Jake leaned his right shoulder against the edge, crossing his arms. He couldn't stop the smile from growing as he watched Vickie jump around while singing into a whisk. Her high ponytail swung with each movement.

Leaping to the side, her bare feet landed hard on the worn carpet, rattling the thin walls. His grin grew. She had always hated wearing shoes, much to her mother's horror.

Vickie spun around and screamed. One hand over her chest and breathing hard, she threw the whisk at him.

Laughing, he ducked and the silver utensil went sailing out the open door.

"Jake Torres! That's not funny. You scared me to death."

"You left your door unlocked, but please don't stop on my account." Closing the door, he moved farther into her living room. He paused and surveyed the small space. "Wow, the trailer looks the same as it did when I lived here, but I don't remember it being so small."

Vickie walked to the counter and turned the volume down. "Yeah, well, you realize you're, like, one hundred times bigger now?" She tried to suppress a giggle. "Back then I was taller than you."

He savored the sound he'd been denied for so many years. "We were ten." He tapped his knuckles on the old counter that separated the galley kitchen from the living area. "I can't believe your dad still has this old thing with the original furniture."

"I'm saving up my money to buy us a house. No reason to waste it on furniture when this works."

He slowly looked over the small living space remembering when this little house had made him feel safe for the first time ever.

A family portrait of Vickie and Tommy with the kids hung on the wall giving Jake a kick in the gut and bringing him back to the present.

Vickie had moved to the other side of the Formica counter and started cleaning. "Daddy had a contract to haul it off when I first moved back." She looked up at him with a gleam in her eye. "My mother just about had a heart attack when I announced I wanted the trailer."

"But your dad gave it to you, anyway."

"Of course. He offered to buy me a new house, but I wanted this one."

"Why?" Jake couldn't keep the skepticism out of his voice.

"Believe it or not, some of my favorite memories with my best friend happened here."

He shot one eyebrow up and stared at her. "Really?"

"Yes, really." She swatted him with the dishrag. "Besides, I need to know I can do this on my own.

Not Daddy or Tommy, but me. I need to do this. I pay rent and everything." Her stubborn chin lifted and she looked him in the eye.

He definitely understood wanting to prove yourself, but she might be going a bit overboard. "So the steps falling in on you or the kids are part of your plan for independence?"

"I noticed they rocked a bit. I thought it was just because they're old." She hesitated. "Can you show me how to fix them?"

"Vickie, I've been known to build and repair whole houses. I think I can manage your steps." He leaned his elbows on the yellow-tinted counter. "It's because they're so old, they probably need to be replaced. I can get it done in less than a day."

"No, *I* can do it. Just tell me what to buy. On second thought, don't bother. I'm sure I can find instructions online and Dannie at Bergmann's Lumberyard can help me."

"Vickie, don't be stubborn. I can give you a list of supplies and one day next week when we're both off I can show you how to build steps. I think Seth should help. Where is he, anyway?"

"He's with my dad in the horse barns. They should be back any moment." She cleaned the same spot she had already wiped several times. With a heavy sigh, she brought her gaze back up to his. "I'm not sure Seth wants to go to the football thing. I'm kind of making him." She turned away and opened the worn cabinet, gathering two tall glasses in one hand.

The clinking of the ice hitting glass filled the silence. Vickie pulled a pitcher of lemonade from the green refrigerator. She finally started talking again while she focused on pouring the drinks. "Tommy could be…well, not the most encouraging person at the best of times. But when it came to Seth he was …"

She wouldn't look him in the eye as she passed the full glass over to him.

"Remember, I know Tommy." He covered her hand with his, holding her in place until she met his gaze. "Don't make excuses for him."

Pulling her hand back, she shook her head. "I just don't want Seth to get hurt."

"No worries there. Between Pastor John, Rhody and me it's more about fellowship and having fun." He grinned as he swirled the glass, watching the liquid form a tornado with the ice. "Don't get me wrong, we're guys, so it gets competitive, but the egos stay home. Seth'll be fine. It's flag, so no tackling or hitting." Jake took a sip of his drink. "Now, what about those cookies cooling by the stove?"

"What cookies?" She blocked his line of vision and held the spatula up like a weapon. "I don't know what you're talking about."

"Oh, come on, you're killin' me." He knew they would still be warm and gooey. "You know how much I love cookies straight from the oven. I'll let you build the steps all by yourself, and I'll just watch from a distance. Please?"

Squinting, Vickie told herself not to look into his eyes. Whenever he'd managed to make eye contact, she'd never been good at telling him no. "These are for Ashley's horse club." She turned with a sigh and slid one on the stainless-steel spatula. Holding it from him, she glared. "Just one?"

He nodded. "Just one, promise."

She watched him take the chocolate chip cookie. His smile warmed her heart in a way no one else ever could.

He closed his eyes and softly moaned as every morsel disappeared. His jaw worked slowly as her gaze followed the movement of his throat.

He looked back at her. "That tasted amazing." He stood and moved next to her in the small kitchen. Reaching across the stove put him right in her space. "What about one…"

She popped the back of his hand with the spatula. "You promised."

He gave a sigh and stepped back as if he had made a great sacrifice. "Yes, I did."

"I used your mother's recipe." Feeling awkward, she moved to the sink and dumped her ice down the drain. "We ate a great deal of her cookies at this counter or in the barn when you managed to steal some."

Chuckling, Jake nodded. "She refuses to make

them for me anymore. Not until I give her grand-children. Parental emotional blackmail at it's worst."

"Why don't you?"

"What?" He blinked.

*Whatever.* She knew better. Today she was in the mood to push him. He's the one that left her and then never got married. "Start a family of your own? You'd make an awesome father."

He shrugged, intensely focused on his drink. "Never felt right. I was on the move with the marines, and then focused on my law-enforcement career. Now working with the church keeps me busy and there seems to be a great deal of kids without fathers in their lives."

Well, that put her in her place, since her own kids were pretty much fatherless. She started stacking the cookies in an airtight container.

She stopped and turned to the radio. A giddy feeling made her heart bubble. "Jake, it's our song!"

His brows shot up in a question. "I didn't know we had a song."

Hands on her hips she shook her head at his cluelessness. "As chair of the prom committee, I selected the song for the king and queen dance. I knew we had received the most votes." A sad smile formed. "I picked it for us."

His forehead wrinkled. "You danced it with Tommy."

"'Cause *you* never showed up." She pointed the spatula at him. *"You* had the most votes. *You* were voted king. Because you weren't there I had to dance with Tommy."

He dared raise his eyebrows and give her a stunned look. "I didn't show up? I waited for two hours under the bridge. You told me you would meet me at Second Crossing Bridge. I was so worried I finally went to your house. Your mother took great pleasure in telling me you went with Tommy. What did you expect me to do?"

"Mother surprised me with Tommy and a limo." She turned away from him and looked out the window. She had been such a coward. She needed to stop blaming her choices on her mother. "I didn't tell her I was meeting you. She never told me you came by the house. It should've been our dance." The last sentence dropped to a whisper, her chest tight. Silence and sadness surrounded her. The ticking of the old clock erased the years.

She felt the warmth of his presence as he moved closer to her. He stopped two steps away from where she stood.

"We could dance it now." His voice low.

She looked over her shoulder. The half grin eased the hardness of his face and the pain in her chest.

"Miss Victoria Lawson, may I have this dance?"

She turned toward him. He stood so gallant, hand out to her, waiting. One heartbeat, two, she hesitated. With a deep sigh, she made a step forward and put her hand in his.

One quick turn and he had them out of the

kitchen and in the living room. An arm placed at her waist gently guided her through the small gap. His strong hand intertwined with her fingers. He led her in a tight circle around the old coffee table.

She closed her eyes and the dingy trailer slipped away. A million tiny white lights filled the new space in her vision. The soft material of her long gown swirled around her legs.

Hanging on to the moment, she took in all the details of the night they should have experienced. "Why didn't you come to the dance?" she whispered, afraid to break the mood but needing to know the answer.

"I did." His voice low and hoarse. "You were dancing with Tommy." Another turn as the music faded. "I figured you'd made your choice."

It was her fault? "I think Mama might have known I was going with you and set it up to make sure I went with Tommy, instead. I thought I would ditch him and find you." They stood face-to-face in the current reality, no music to transport here to another time. "When you didn't show, I thought you had given up on me."

He pressed his forehead against the top of hers.

Vickie remained still, listening to him breathe. Afraid, she kept her eyes closed, head down. "Do you ever wonder where we would be today if I had stood up to my mother and gone with you?"

Jake's strong hands cupped her jaw and brought her gaze up to meet his dark chocolate eyes. "We were so young." He gave her his best half grin. "And maybe a bit dumb. I don't know what would have happened."

She leaned forward and closed her eyes. "You left town, and I was so impatient and couldn't wait to start my family. Now I'm a full-fledged, messed-up adult with two kids to raise. We can't get this right, can we?"

Jake held her face in his large hands, tilting her head up. He studied her eyes with the most forceful look she had ever seen in him. Her throat went dry as he moved in closer. His stare now focused on her lips. She stopped breathing, his head lowered. His breath, sweet from the lemonade caressed her skin.

Ashley threw the front door open and burst into the room. "Mommy! Mommy!"

Jake jumped back and coughed.

Vickie couldn't stop the giggle that sprang from her wrecked nerves. She blinked a couple of times to refocus.

"What is it, sweetheart?" She wrapped her arms around Ashley's shoulders as her daughter collided into her. Determined to settle her stomach down, Vickie forced a smile.

"Papa Jack's favorite mare had its foal last night and we got to see it and touch it. It has a blond coat, like me. She is so pretty. I'm so in love with her."

"I imagine she fell in love with you, too." She stroked her daughter's hair back from her face.

"I think she did. She tried following me out. Her

legs are so long." Ashley turned and faced Jake, now sitting on a bar stool at the counter. "Hello, Officer Torres."

Seth followed a bit slower and much to Vickie's surprise, he almost wore a smile, reminding her of the boy she used to know. "Hey, Seth, so did you enjoy the horses, too?"

He shrugged. "Yeah, Papa Jack said he can start teaching me to rope. If it's all right with you."

Her father walked in behind the kids with a concerned look on his face. "Vickie, why didn't you tell me the steps were about to collapse?"

"Daddy, they're not that bad, and I'm taking care of it."

Crossing the small room, Jackson Walker Lawson, the fourth, called J.W. by everyone but his daughter and grandchildren, shook Jake's hand.

"Crazy, stubborn girl. I should have come over earlier to make sure it was livable."

"It's livable, Daddy. It just needs a little work." She waved a hand toward Jake without looking at him. There was no way she could make eye contact with him now and not fall apart. "Jake has offered to teach Seth and me to build steps." She turned to Seth. "Doesn't that sound fun, building something with our own hands?"

He shrugged again. "I guess."

Jake stood. "Hey, Seth, are you ready to play some football?"

Seth shoved his hands in his pockets and dropped

his head. "I don't know. I'm not very good. The whole throwing or catching the ball thing seems to be too hard for me."

Jake stood. "Hey, me, too."

Seth shot him a classic teenager skeptical glare. "Really?"

"Yeah, that's why I like chasing down the guys with the football."

Confusion shadowed his eyes. "If you don't have the ball, why bother playing?"

Vickie bit her lip. That sounded every bit like Tommy's glorious words of self-righteous wisdom.

Jake's jaw went hard. "Football is a team sport, Seth. You don't have a real game without protectors and defenders."

J.W. walked over to Seth and patted his back. "Don't worry about what your dad said, son. You're almost twelve and growing fast. At your age I could barely walk without tripping." He gave Vickie and Ashley a hug. "I'm heading out. Call me if you need anything. Love you."

She kissed him on the cheek. "Love you, too, Daddy."

"See you later, Jake."

"Sir." Jake gave him a nod. After the door closed, her childhood friend stood with his hands in his pockets, keeping his gaze on Seth. "Well, I guess we'll head out. I should have him back between four and four-thirty."

"I'll come pick him up, no need for you to drive all the way out here. What time is it over?"

"We're usually done before four, but it's pretty informal, so he can leave whenever you get there."

"Okay, sounds good."

They stood there like idiots not wanting to leave but not having any reason to stay.

"Are we going or not?" Insolence laced Seth's voice.

"Seth!" Embarrassed at his attitude, Vickie sent an apologetic glance to Jake.

"It's okay." Jake patted the sullen teen on the back. "I'm ready for some football." With a wink to Vickie, he followed Seth out the door.

That wink made her feel things she needed to pack away with her homecoming mums. She wanted to be independent. She *needed* to be independent. Instead, he made her consider giving it all up to hide in his arms. Coming home, she would have never guessed Jake Torres would be the biggest threat to her sanity and heart.

# Chapter Six

Vickie pulled into the gravel parking lot of the unfinished youth building. Her daughter leaped out of the car before she shut off the engine. Racing across the field, Ashley stopped at the sideline and started jumping up and down, cheering for her brother. Vickie chuckled at the look of horror on Seth's face.

With a smile, she grabbed the extra cookies she and Ashley had made after Jake had left with Seth. Making her way across the dry field, Vickie kept her gaze on Jake. She stopped next to her daughter.

A mix of men and boys ranging in age from twelve to fifty made up the teams; her son looked to be the youngest. Seth crouched down next to Jake, his fingers in the dusty ground as they made up the line. His stare fixed on her boss, Rhody Buchannan. The Mercantile owner played quarterback for the other team. The ball snapped, and Vickie held her breath. Seth looked so small out there with the men and high school boys.

Rhody handed the ball off to Derrick De La Soto, a teenager in the youth band. Jake cut him off, forcing him toward Seth. Her heart froze, and she shot a quick prayer for her son. Seth pounced and gripped the bright yellow flag from Derrick's hip. He jumped up with the flag high in the air. Ashley yelled his name and clapped.

With a huge sigh of relief, Vickie released the death grip on the container of cookies. Pastor John blew a whistle and called the game. The teams started mingling and shaking hands. Seth ran toward her, his hair sweaty and plastered to his skin.

"Mom, did you see what I did?"

His blue eyes sparkled in a way she had not seen in the last two years.

"Yes, I'm so proud of you." *I will not cry.*

Pastor John walked over and patted Seth on the back. "Great job today, Seth. I'm glad you joined us."

"Thank you for letting me play. Mom, I got five flags." He bounced on the balls of his feet.

"I think we might have created a defensive monster," the pastor said.

"Yeah, they couldn't get through us. We built a solid wall. I love football, Mom. Dad just had me in the wrong positions." He glanced at the box in her hand. "Can I have a cookie?"

"Oh, yes. Here, Pastor. I brought your favorite, chocolate chip pecan." She held out the container, allowing each to take one.

"Can I take them to the teams?"

"That's why I brought them."

Seth ran off with the cookies, and Ashley followed. Jake had worked wonders in one afternoon.

The pastor pulled her out of her own thoughts. "Seth and Jake seem to be getting along well. Seth's coming out of his shell."

She nodded. "I'm so sorry for the problems he caused with Rachel and well…" She had to say the words no matter how humiliating. "Pastor John…"

"Vickie, it's okay. Seth apologized, too." He gave her a lopsided grin. "I did tell Rachel if she ever left the house without permission again, she would be grounded until she turned thirty. Raising children is a rough job, and doing it as a single parent is even harder. Remember, you don't have to do it alone. The church is here for you."

She swallowed the burning knot lodged in her throat. "Thank you, but it's more than Seth's behavior. I had no excuse for the way I treated Lorrie Ann."

John rested his hand on her shoulder. "It's behind us." He nodded and smiled. "Asking for forgiveness is difficult, but sometimes accepting it is even more so."

Vickie wrapped her arms around her middle.

"Thank you so much for everything." Pulling her gaze from her son and Jake, she looked at Pastor John. "So now I'm making the dresses for your wedding. How are the rest of the plans coming along?"

He groaned. "Don't get me wrong. I'm so happy Lorrie Ann has been able to reconnect with her mother and wants to involve Sonia while also respecting Maggie as the mother that raised her, but convoluted would not be an exaggeration. Throw in her cousin Yolanda and my two girls and you have total chaos. Lorrie Ann reassures me it is controlled chaos, but I'm not sure I'm buying it."

He popped a green Jolly Rancher in his mouth. "We're trying to keep it small, but everyone in town seems to think they also have a say. Lorrie Ann is excited about the ideas she has for you."

A little bit of shock still stumbled through her at the thought of making the dresses for Lorrie Ann's wedding. For a while she had thought dating Pastor Levi would be a perfect way to get over Tommy. He had made it clear he wasn't interested.

The minute Lorrie Ann stepped back into town, Vickie could tell John reconsidered his stance on dating. That had stung her pride.

Then Jake defended Lorrie Ann, and Vickie had gone right back to high school and picked up the role of the mean girl again. The list of things for which she needed to ask forgiveness seemed to be getting longer instead of shorter.

She could do this. "Maybe Lorrie Ann needs to find someone else. I know a woman in Uvalde that…"

"Lorrie Ann wants you, and Maggie is determined that you make her and Sonia's dresses, too. Lorrie Ann was amazed with your work on the costumes at the Christmas pageant. Don't let past mistakes or fear stop you from using your gifts."

A flash of guilt caused her to bite the inside of her cheek. She had almost ruined the Christmas pageant because she had been jealous of Lorrie Ann. "Thank you. I do love sewing."

Embarrassment had her wanting to hide, but she had already agreed and she owed Lorrie Ann so much. "Well, the thought of designing dresses for the whole party is exciting." She looked over the brown football field. Jake had two cookies in his hand. He saluted her and mouthed his thanks, winking before turning back to the huddle of males.

"Pastor John, I have a question," she said as she focused on the hills surrounding the little valley.

"What can I help you with?" The steadiness and concern in his voice calmed her.

"How do we know God's plan for us? I mean, how can we tell the difference between what *we* want and what *God* wants for us?"

"That's always a tough question. If it's driven by doubt, guilt, fear or a long list of other negative emotions, it's not God. God is love without fear."

He touched her shoulder to bring her gaze back to him.

"Vickie, find some scriptures that mean something to you and pray on them. Sometimes we are so afraid of change, we tune God out." He gave her one of his lopsided smiles. "I've been guilty of that and almost lost my chance with Lorrie Ann."

Vickie sighed and looked back over the field at all the male bonding. Jake turned and grinned. Saying a few words, he left the group and started walking toward them.

"Vickie, God doesn't guilt you or manipulate you into a relationship with him. People will, but God wants you to be there of your own free will. Everything else will fall into place."

She had done her best to manipulate everyone around her because of her own misery. In the end, Pastor John and Lorrie Ann's love had won the day. Now she needed to grow up and focus on loving her children.

Pastor John's voice pulled her back to him. "Jake's a good man."

"Yes, he is, but we both know I've never been known for being a good or kind woman."

"Vickie, you were made in the image of God. Sometimes all the other voices confuse us and take us off the path God intended. But that doesn't mean you can't get back on, sometimes with even a greater understanding of our purpose."

Pastor John had always believed in her even when she didn't deserve it.

Jake joined them and slapped John on the shoulder. "Good game today, John." He turned to her. "Vickie, thanks for the cookies." He pushed his hair back and smiled. "Seth did great today."

"Thank you so much for bringing him. I haven't seen him this excited about anything in a while."

"I'll see y'all later." Pastor John jogged across the field and talked to the players as they started to leave.

Seth ran over to her, followed by Ashley, his voice high with excitement. "Mom, can we go to the drugstore? Some of the guys are going to get a soda. They invited me. Can I go?"

Jake's knees popped as he sat on his heels next to Ashley. "You want to go? I'll treat you and your mom to a Coke float."

Now her daughter was jumping around. It had been a while since they had gone out. "Mommy, please?"

Jake stood and gave her his best smile. "How about it?"

She had promised herself to keep her distance from Jake, but she looked at the kids, their faces glowing. "Okay."

Seth whooped and ran back to the small group of teenage boys.

"I'm so glad to see him making friends." She was doing this for Seth. "Since moving back, Rachel seemed to be the only friend he had, and I don't think Pastor John was too happy about it."

Jake laughed and tossed the football to Ashley. "I can't imagine any father being happy about boys hanging around his daughter."

Jake found himself smiling. He buried the urge to take Vickie's hand as they walked toward the cars. Seth had taken the ball from his sister and tossed it in the air, talking nonstop. All the while, Ashley walked next to Vickie, teasing her brother. Vickie laughed at one of his replies, and it was all Jake could do to not pull her into his arms. This felt so right.

He dreamed of having this family when he allowed his dreams to go there.

Seth bounded into his truck, and they followed Vickie's Ford to the Main Street Drugstore. He noticed the tires were new.

They pulled into parking spots in front of the strip of buildings, and the kids were out and running through the door before Vickie climbed out of her little car.

He waited at the bottom of the giant concrete step that led to the wide sidewalk. She put her hands into her pockets when he reached out to help her up. She gave him a faint smile and walked past him to the store.

Lined in chrome, the drugstore's long counter reflected its glory days from the 1940s. Round barstools padded with red vinyl took the tourists and locals back to a sweeter time.

Ashley stood by the glass door with a pout, glaring at her brother. Seth sat at the back of the diner in a corner booth with some of the other boys on the team. "Seth won't let me sit with him."

Jake put his hand on her shoulder. "Come on, you can sit with us. Those boys are smelly, anyway." They made their way to a side booth. "Do you want a Coke float or a shake?"

Ashley followed her mother onto the bench across from him. Before answering, she looked at her mom. "Can I have a pink shake, Mommy?"

Vickie grabbed her red purse.

"I've got it." Jake smiled at the server as she walked over. "Hey, Cassie. Could you add Seth to my tab when he orders?"

"Sure, no problem." She smiled back and flipped her little pad. "So what can I get you, Officer Torres?"

A frown pulled on Vickie's face as she fussed with her purse. "I can get ours."

"I told you it was my treat." Turning back to Cassie Walters, he continued. "One strawberry shake, one chocolate, a Coke float and a large order of chili-cheese fries."

Ashley clapped. "I love those, but we never get 'em!"

"Jake," Vickie said in a stern voice.

He had to give her credit for her no-nonsense

tone, but he ignored it anyway and winked at Ashley. "Your mom loved the chili-cheese fries, but I don't think she was allowed to eat them. After school, I would order a big dish so she could sneak a few."

Vickie glared at him then went back to fighting with her bag.

As Cassie turned to leave, her son, a dark-haired boy of about four ran over. "Officer Torres! I drew a picture for you." He held out a paper filled with colorful figures.

"I'm so sorry." His mother gave them a sheepish half smile as she started to pull the little boy away. "Bryce, I told you to stay at the table."

Jake patted the little boy's shoulder. "It's okay. Bryce man, let me see your picture."

The chubby hand held up his artwork. "It's you and your police car. See there's Mommy and me at our new house you took us to. I even have King, our dog, right here. And I still have Teddy." Tucked under his arm was a floppy teddy bear. Bryce laid the picture on the table in front of Jake. "I made the picture for you."

In big red letters the words, "THANK YOU," ran across the top of the paper.

Ruffling the boy's hair, he glanced up at Cassie. "Glad to hear you like the new place. Everything good?"

She nodded. "Yeah. Thank you for all your help." She guided Bryce back to his table littered with books, paper and colors. "I'll have your order right out."

Vickie's knuckles strained from the grip she had on the leather strap of her purse. For a brief second, a haunted look crossed her face.

"You always find a way of helping the underdog, don't you?"

He didn't understand the tinge of bitterness covered by a bit of awe.

He shrugged. "It's my job." He needed to find a way to change the subject.

"Look, Mommy." Ashley bounced in the bench, causing the old springs to squeak. She had the sugar packets lined up.

"Sit, Ashley." Vickie pulled a storybook out of her purse. "Here, sweetheart."

"Oh, do you have my pictures?"

Vickie went back to digging in her purse and pulled a small photo album from the huge bag.

"What else do you have in that bag?" Jake asked.

A soft laugh passed her lips. "When Seth was little, I learned to keep things on hand to entertain them."

"Mommy helped me make my own story. These are my favorite pictures." She hopped over to his side of the table and opened her book. "Here's me and Seth on the first day of school in Clear Water. Seth didn't want his picture taken. He was mad." She made sure Jake saw the picture. "I was five, and Mommy tried not to cry."

Jake smiled at Vickie with a raised brow. She rolled her eyes and shook her head. Ashley flipped the album to the next picture.

"Here's one on the day I was born. I'm in the incubator like a baby chick. Me-Maw and Papa Jack were there. I came early so Daddy missed it. The doctors told Mommy I might not live, but I did." With a big smile, she looked at her mother. "I'm special, right?"

Vickie reached across the table and tucked a wild strand of hair behind her daughter's ear. "Yes, you are." With a bit of hardness in her eyes she looked at Jake for the first time since the game. "That's when Tommy was running for State Senate. I messed up his timetable when I went into labor five weeks before schedule."

Jake managed to smile at her, but he hated to imagine how scared she must have been. *How could Tommy not be there for his family?* He probably blamed her when he lost the political race, too.

He glanced at the miniature Vickie sitting next to her. With a front tooth missing, Ashley's grin melted his heart. He sighed. Not a good time to say what he thought of Tommy.

A large serving tray balanced on her left hand, Cassie set their order on the table. Vickie stared at her frosty glass with a huge scoop of ice cream floating in the dark soda. Her eyes closed as she sipped on the straw.

Forgetting her picture album, Ashley stabbed

a fork into the mountain of cheese and chili piled high on top of crispy, home-cut fries.

Vickie picked up a fork and carefully selected a fry, making sure all the good stuff coated the fried potato. He might have even heard a moan as she chewed. He took a gulp of his own chocolate shake.

Ashley tapped his arm and pointed to another photo. "Oh, here's Mommy and Daddy dancing at their wedding." Jake gave the little girl a tight smile. He glanced at the picture then turned away. That was one photo he hoped never to see again.

He looked at Vickie and found her watching Seth. "He's fine, Vickie."

"Oh, I know but as a mother you never stop worrying. Some of those boys are older, and one is Tommy's cousin's kid."

Ashley stayed focused on her book. "Mommy was a cheerleader her first year at college."

Jake looked at the beautiful girl in the dark green uniform. Standing on the shoulders of some guy, she had her fist high in the air. "Why did you drop out of college?"

She shrugged. "I wanted to be a mother more than I wanted to be a fashion designer."

"Mommy designed her own prom dress." Ashley flipped through a couple of pages until she found the one she wanted. "Look how beautiful she is with her crown. Her and Daddy were the king and queen."

"Actually, your father was runner-up. Jake had won but didn't show up, so they gave it to your dad."

The group of boys walked past them, some stopping to say goodbye to Jake. Seth slid into the booth next to his mother.

"You have that stupid book out again?" Seth grumbled as he picked up a chili-drenched fry.

"Seth!" Vickie scolded between clenched teeth.

Jake wasn't sure if it was the rudeness to Ashley or the lack of table manners that appalled her most.

Ashley ignored her brother and unfortunately stayed focused on the old prom picture. "If you had won, why didn't you go to the prom?" Ashley frowned at him. She looked so much like her mother he had to smile.

He shrugged. "I was under a bridge waiting for my date."

Seth shook his head and sucked air through his straw. "And she never showed? Oh, man, you got stood up. Who was she. Do we know her?"

Jake shook his head. "It doesn't matter, old history."

Vickie picked at her napkin. "I think if you asked her today she'd regret doing it."

Ashley looked up from her pictures. "You know her, Mommy? Well, that was mean." The injustice of it apparently bothered Ashley a great deal. She turned back to Jake. "Did you buy a beautiful corsage for her?"

Jake grinned at the little girl's pout. "I did. I

spent a whole week's paycheck on it." He winked at Vickie as she squirmed in her chair. Good.

Ashley plopped back on the red vinyl booth, her arms crossed. "Well, it was just wrong."

Vickie stared into her empty old-fashioned Coke glass. "Yes, it was."

Seth snorted and nodded in understanding. "Maybe her parents didn't like you. I know how that feels. Pastor John wouldn't let Rachel go to the Homecoming dance with me."

"You're both too young, anyway," Vickie scolded him.

"Mom! I'm not a kid." His jaw tightened.

"Seth." She gave him her best mom stare.

Ashley moved closer to Jake. "So her mom didn't like you? Why?"

Jake reached over and wiped a smudge of melted cheese off Ashley's cheek. "It gets complicated. And there are blessings to be found in any path we take." He looked Vickie straight in the eyes.

Looking at her two blessings, Vickie bit her bottom lip and nodded. As much as she regretted her marriage to Tommy, she couldn't ever imagine her life without Seth and Ashley. "Yes." She took a deep breath. "I'll be right back." She darted to the back of the drugstore.

Seth turned, and Ashley got on her knees to watch her mom.

"Is she okay?" Ashley looked concerned.

"I'm sure she just had to go to the restroom. Hey,

last call before your mother gets back. Who wants something to drink?"

Before they could order, Vickie returned. "So y'all ready to head home?" She picked up her purse and threw a five on the table. "Thank you for everything, Jake. This was a great day."

The kids scooted out and headed to the door. Vickie turned to follow them, but Jake laid a hand on her arm. "Would you like to go out this weekend for dinner, maybe after you build your steps?"

"Jake, right now I need to focus on the kids..."

"We can do something all together, putt-putt golf or a movie. I like spending time with your kids." He was desperate to find a way to stop her from saying no.

"Jake, I can't, not yet."

"Okay." He stepped back. "I'll drop a list for you at Bergmann's Lumberyard later today. They can help you gather the supplies for the stairs."

"Thank you." She paused for a moment, and Jake held his breath; maybe she'd change her mind. Instead, she turned and followed her children out of the drugstore. With the opening and closing of the glass door, the chime went off.

The cheery little bell mocked his loneliness as Jake watched the life he wanted walk out into the street and drive away.

## Chapter Seven

Vickie pulled small squares of scrap material out of the cardboard box. The familiar smells of the fellowship hall, lemon cleaner and lingering coffee helped her focus. Anything to stop the internal debate from replaying in her head.

Should she or should she not take Jake up on his offer of a date?

Soon the new sewing club would start, and the fellowship hall would be full of children. That was the plan, anyway. She hoped more than her two and Pastor John's girls would show up. She wasn't sure if anyone in town would trust her to teach their kids about giving and sharing.

Lorrie Ann thought Tuesday after school would be the best time for their new mission project.

Which was good because she planned to stay away Wednesday night. Jake almost always attended the prayer meeting. Ugh…she was doing it again.

Did thinking about not thinking about Jake count as thinking about him? She was going crazy.

"Mom, where do you want these?" Seth walked in, followed by Rachel, Celeste and Ashley. Each carried a box filled with the little pieces of leftover multicolored material.

Thankful for something to stop the turning of her hamster wheel, she moved her now-empty box under the table. "Right here. Thanks, guys." She glanced down the hall. "Where's Lorrie Ann?"

Rachel answered. "She went back to the office to get the other supplies."

Seth looked around. "Where's the sewing machines?"

"There aren't any."

He turned back to her. Confusion marred his face. "Then how are y'all going to sew the bears together?"

With a grin, she went back to pulling scraps out. "We are going to sew them by hand."

"Oh, good luck with that." He shook his head.

Rachel paused in her work and looked at Seth. "You're not staying?"

"Well…I hadn't…" He crossed his arms and shrugged his shoulders. "Do you want me to stay?"

Vickie rolled her eyes. "I thought you were going to open gym at the school."

Celeste giggled. "You could make matching love bears for each other."

Rachel glared at her little sister. "Maybe you should have gone with Daddy."

"Girls, you're not fighting, are you?" Lorrie Ann walked into the room, a large bag in each hand.

Head lowered, Celeste muttered. "No, ma'am."

At the same time, Rachel said, "She's embarrassing me."

Trying not to laugh, Vickie took the bags from Lorrie Ann. The back door opened, and Adrian and his daughter, Mia, walked into the room. The girls ran to Mia and greeted her, pulling her to their table.

Adrian held his black cowboy hat in his hands. "She's been very excited about this. She was going to have to go to my job site tonight, so thanks for inviting her." With a quick goodbye, he left. A couple more girls came in and joined the group.

Vickie was surprised to see Katy Buchannan walk in with her youngest son, Colt, and his friend Carlos. The boys stood there until Celeste pulled them over to the girls.

"Hi, Vickie. Lorrie Ann." Katy hugged them both. "Colt was so thrilled about this but none of his brothers would come, so he convinced Carlos to join him."

"Oh, that's great. I think Seth is staying, too." She glanced at her boss's wife, who also happened to be the closest person she had to a friend. Vickie hoped the look she gave her had just the right amount of desperation. She hated to ask for help. "Are you staying?"

Katy's moment of wide-eyed shock was followed by an easy smile. "You're asking me to help? Sure. I never learned to sew myself, but I'm good at kid control."

When Vickie heard the door, she lost her breath for a moment. Jake held it open. In his free hand, he had a large, overstuffed quilted bag. With the sound of a familiar thump, Vickie's stomach tightened.

Moving to the door, she braced herself for the reason. Tommy's great-aunt, Mrs. Miller, a.k.a. Dragon Lady, had decided to grace their new club with her presence. What brought Mrs. Miller to their little sewing project?

Jake dared to smile at her. Laughter flickered in his face. "I found Mrs. Miller on the side of the road. Her car broke down, but she demanded I bring her here." He winked at her. "She said you needed her help."

Vickie glanced at Lorrie Ann, but she shrugged her shoulders.

"I am on the mission board, you know." The older lady shot a glare at Lorrie Ann. "If we started a new outreach project I should have been told."

Poor Lorrie Ann started playing with her new engagement ring. "We weren't using church funds so I didn't think I needed to bother anyone."

Vickie stepped forward to get the attention on her. "I wanted to help and all I have is sewing."

"Yes, well, you did always think you could do whatever you wanted. Thankfully, JoAnn called me to let me know what you were up to." She pointed to the table covered in scraps of material. "Put my bag there, young man." She made a pointed look at Lorrie Ann. "You are Pastor John's helpmate now, and you have to be more responsible."

"Yes, ma'am." Lorrie Ann turned to her bags. "I have the sewing kits."

Jake set the overstuffed bag next to Vickie and leaned in close.

His whisper tickled her ear. "Sorry. I tried to convince her we needed to get her car fixed, but she refused to do anything other than come here and save y'all."

Checking the bag, she started going through the beautiful scraps of material. "I don't envy the scrutiny Lorrie Ann is about to find herself in as the future wife of Pastor John."

A low, deep chuckle rumbled from Jake. "I wonder if she's having doubts about marrying a preacher in a small town."

Vickie nodded. "Being a pastor's wife might be worse than being a wannabe politician's wife." She shuddered. She never wanted to go through that again.

A couple of Rachel's friends joined them along with Yolanda, Lorrie Ann's cousin. By the time it started, she counted thirteen kids and six adults.

Taking the scraps over to the group of children,

Vickie showed them the first steps of sewing the small pieces together, in order to have a large enough square to make the bear.

The kids rushed the area with all the donated scraps and picked their favorite colors and patterns. Lorrie Ann and Jake passed out the little sewing kits. Katy, Yolanda and Mrs. Miller helped any of the children struggling. Laughter and joy filled the room as they all set to work on the first step to their patchwork teddy bears.

Carlos stayed behind picking up one piece only to put it down and pick up another. His dark eyes squinted as he studied the choices.

"Don't worry about which ones you pick. Any color and pattern you choose will work." Vickie gathered four random squares for her own little bear. "See, now I'll sew them together."

He sighed. "But I thought we were making these for Officer Torres." He glanced up at the man beside her. "They're for kids in bad places, right? They might even be crying. I want mine to be perfect for them."

Jake sat on his heels, coming eye to eye with the six-year-old. "My sister has a teddy bear like the one you're going to make. You know what makes it perfect?"

The little boy shook his head, his eyes larger than the big buttons brought to embellish the stuffed bears.

"That someone cared enough to give her one

when she needed something to hug close to her. The bear made by your hands will give the little boy or girl a smile."

Vickie joined them on ground level with four patterned squares of different colors. "Will these work for you? The blues, brown and green make a nice combination. You can add more to it after we put the bear together."

Taking the material, Carlos nodded his head and joined the other kids.

Jake offered his hand to her as he stood. "You know, at this rate you're going to ruin your reputation as an Ice Queen."

She laughed softly. "That's the point. I feel I owe everyone an apology, not just Lorrie Ann." Her gaze found Seth and Ashley in the midst of the other children. "It's nice to really help and not just worry about how it appears. I want my kids to be proud of their mom."

Jake took a moment to study her. The girl he played with on the ranch wavered before him. The side of Vickie no one else knew was making its first public appearance. "You're doing great. I know from firsthand experience how important something like these bears can be to a frightened child."

Giving him her full attention, Vickie stepped closer, her voice low. "Really? When did your sister get one? Does it have to do with how you lost your dad?"

He saw the questions in her eyes. The answers

weren't his to give. "It was before we came to Clear Water." He looked away, needing a new subject. His brain came up empty.

Vickie laid her hand on his arm. "Growing up, it was always about me, wasn't it? I don't remember ever talking about you."

He held a steady gaze as she searched his eyes, not sure what she looked for.

She leaned in, melancholy clouding her deep green irises. "I just realized…" Her soft voice was raspy. "I know nothing about you before you showed up at the ranch with your mom and sister. Man, have I always been so selfish? I'm so sorry."

The desire to remove any unhappiness from her expression always motivated him more than any of his own sadness. He patted her hand that rested on his sleeve. "I didn't want to talk about me. I wanted to ride horses up the hill, jump in the river and spend hours looking at the sky. I loved being around you and listening to your voice. You would talk about your sisters, friends, mother and your father. You had such a full and exciting life."

"You're a good man, Jake Torres." She didn't look any happier.

"I try to be." Sometimes he wondered if it was enough to erase the bad he had done. "Victoria, you are doing a great thing here. Think what a difference it will make when I tell a terrified child this little bear was made just for them."

She picked up a stack of papers. Joy finally

rested on her lips. "Well, the bears won't make themselves. I need to take the patterns to them." She leaned across the table. "I should thank you for bringing Mrs. Miller, but I haven't reached that level of graciousness yet." She glanced back to the happy little group sewing away. "I'm sure she will find the opportunity to advise me on how to be a good wife. She and my mother played the same recording." With a heavy sigh and a grin, she headed toward the table filled with children.

Jake grabbed some squares and followed.

She looked over her shoulder and raised her eyebrows. "Are you staying?"

He shrugged. "Sure. Why not?"

"I thought football and roping were more your style."

"I've been known to enjoy other activities. Seth is here. Might as well show him real men do more than play sports." He winked and sat down next to Ashley, asking her how to do the first step. For a minute, Vickie just stared at him. He took the moment to enjoy the confusion in her eyes. He gave her another wink.

She jumped in the middle of the group and demonstrated cutting the pattern while talking about how these bears will help other kids. They would each pick a scripture to place in the bear. The next couple of hours she taught and guided, until a dozen colorful teddy bears lined the table.

Was it possible to love her again? The thought

terrified him, remembering how much it hurt losing her the first time. Could he survive that pain twice?

The next morning, Jake scanned the line of trucks and SUVs parked in front of the diner. The usual Wednesday breakfast crowd.

A layer of dust covered everything, even the wooden arrow with the words "Fast Food 90 miles that way" hand-painted on it. Jake spotted Sheriff Johnson's Land Rover next to a tan truck with the Childress Cutting Horses logo that belonged to Dub Childress.

Dub was also John's father-in-law from his first marriage. Jake wondered how it felt to be connected to so many people; in small towns it was more like three degrees of separation. He just had his mom and sister.

Vickie's dad, J.W., the sheriff and Dub had asked him to meet them at the Rio Canyon Café. He parked alongside the Lawson Ranch truck. What did the unofficial town elders want with him?

Nerves as tight as a kid called into the principal's office, Jake walked through the door and noticed the three men in their regular corner booth. The place was packed with customers, and coffee and bacon aromas filled the popular breakfast spot.

Maybe Seth had done something, but having Dub Childress here didn't make sense. People greeted him. He stopped a few times to ask about family members or hear comments on the drought.

When he finally made it to the round table, J.W. scooted in a bit to make room for him. The blinds behind them were closed to block the morning sun. Each man had a large white cup of coffee.

"Glad you could make it, Jake." The sheriff yelled toward the back. "Becca, we're ready."

A tiny brunette came out from behind the wood lattice screen. Rebecca Delgado held a coffeepot in one hand and a cup in the other. Setting the cup down in front of Jake, she pulled two cream packets out of her apron. "Hi, Officer Torres, aren't you a bit young to be joining the breakfast club?"

Dub raised one brow at her. "Hey, girl, I'll tell your mother you're harassing your best customers."

She rolled her eyes and poured fresh coffee in each of their cups. "So the usual all around?" She looked at Jake and smiled. "What can I get you?"

Before he could answer, Dub interrupted. "I think I want to try something different this morning. Any new specials?"

J.W. and Sheriff Johnson both sighed as Dub had Becca go through the menu and fresh baked goods. He nodded and asked about substitutes and then ordered his usual.

J.W. glanced at Jake. "He does that every time, then orders the same thing he's ordered for the last ten years.

"I might want something new. One of these days I will. It's good to think about stirrin' things up."

Shaking his head, Jake placed his order.

Dub continued talking. "I tell you what. This drought is hitting me hard. If it lasts much longer, I'll be selling half my herd."

The sheriff took a sip of his coffee. "It's so dry. We'd go up like a tinder box with one spark."

J.W. ran his hand through his graying hair. "At this rate it's heading to be the worst on record."

Jake frowned. Surely, they hadn't called him in to discuss the weather. So did he just wait them out or say something?

The sheriff spoke next, looking at J.W. "So how's your grandson recovering from his ordeal?"

"He's good. We came so close to losing him, but seeing the boy now, you'd have no clue he'd been near death." He nodded to Jake. "Jake, here, took him out to play football. He caught five flags." He glanced over at Jake. "By the way, thanks for taking him. He needs more strong role models."

The respect in J.W.'s eyes moved Jake.

The sheriff pointed a finger at Jake. "You did a great job that night." He nodded before going back to his coffee. "You had the volunteers out and organized by the time I got out of bed."

"That was Maggie. And Lorrie Ann is the one that found the kids." Okay, so this was good or maybe it was the positive before they hit him with bad news.

"Yes, but you kept everyone organized and focused. That takes true leadership skills," Dub added between his own sips of coffee.

With plates balanced along her arm, Becca set his breakfast in front of him. He smiled, grateful for the interruption. He looked at his potato and egg tacos.

It gave him time to compose himself. The praise was overwhelming. Most boys dreamed of making the big play that wins the game. These men were giving him everything he fantasized about while growing up. It was nice to hear that men like these respected his work.

He took a bite, giving himself some time to collect the emotions and put them back into place. One slow swallow before he trusted himself to speak without sounding stupid. "Thank you. That's an honor coming from you."

J.W. spoke next. "I appreciate you watching out for Vickie. She can be a bit stubborn. Are those steps taken care of?"

"She has the materials. I'll be over there in a couple of days to help her replace them."

"Good. I'm proud of the choices she's been making since returning home. You know she's been given the keys to the Mercantile while the Buchannans are on vacation."

Sheriff Johnson squinted. "I don't remember them ever leaving town. They must really trust her." He dipped his biscuit in the white gravy.

"Is that why you asked me here?" Okay, this is about Vickie, but it didn't make sense why he was meeting with all three men. "You want me and the sheriff to serve as extra eyes on the Mercantile?"

"No, she's just real proud of the trust they gave her. That girl is working hard to put her life back together after Tommy steamrolled her. I don't want her thinking I went behind her back to get help for her."

The sheriff pointed his forked sausage at him. "We called you to discuss county business."

Confused, Jake pushed his plate back. "So this is official business?"

J.W. leaned in closer. "Nope, just havin' a friendly discussion among friends." He dragged his last piece of fluffy pancake through the real maple syrup. "Over breakfast."

Becca came by the table. "More coffee?"

Jake covered his cup. "None for me." At this point his nerves were already strung too tight. Jake prayed it wasn't anything unethical; he respected each man and didn't want to lose that. He had heard of the small-town, back-room deals from other officers but hadn't come across any here in Clear Water.

The sheriff crossed his arms and leaned toward Jake. "Here's the deal. I'm ready to spend more time fishing with the grandkids."

His stomach knotted.

"You know the guy from Houston who moved into the Fishers' old place?"

Jake nodded, still confused. Ryan Vanderbilt was

a retired cop from Houston. Recently, Jake stopped him for speeding. He was a little arrogant, but over-all he hadn't caused any problems.

"Well, I've heard through the grapevine he's asking personal questions about me."

"Yeah, like when he's going to retire. He seems to believe our good sheriff here has had the job too long," Dub said.

The sheriff tossed his wadded napkin on his empty plate "Jake, I really don't want to run again, but I can't leave my county to him."

J.W. spoke next. "We want you to run for sheriff. You're one of us. You know this land, the people."

Jake's mind was wiped clear of every thought. Sheriff...they wanted him to be the next sheriff. He looked around the diner. People carried on as if the world hadn't just shifted. He swung his gaze around to the three men and found each looking back at him in question. They waited for an answer.

They saw him as a vital part of the community, someone they trusted to protect it.

"I don't know." *God, what do I do? They don't know me. They don't know what I've done to my own father.* "This is definitely an unexpected honor."

"You're a man of integrity, and it would be our honor to support you as the next sheriff of Rio County."

"I'm not sure I can..."

J.W. put his hand flat out. "Stop. No more words.

We understand this is a big decision. Take some time and pray about it."

Dub flicked his chin over his shoulder. "Well, lookie who just walked in our little café."

Making his way through the tables was the man himself, Ryan Vanderbilt. He laughed aloud at something before moving toward them.

"Hello, gentlemen. It's a great day in Clear Water, Texas. Mind if I join you?" He proceeded to pull up a chair and flipped it backward, straddling the back. "So are you havin' a little meeting of the local law enforcements?"

"Nope, just a breakfast with friends." J.W. took a slow sip of his coffee.

"Well, I wanted to talk to each of you, so all you being here is a great opportunity." He raised his hand and snapped his fingers. "Excuse me. Miss, get me some coffee, would ya? Now what was I sayin'? Yes, I've been doing some research and have found after almost thirty years of service, Sheriff, you might be ready to retire."

Johnson cleared his throat. "Is that so, Vanderbilt?"

"Yes, sir." He paused as Becca set a full cup in front of him.

She pulled two pink packs and one creamer out of her apron and sat them on the table in front of him.

He shook his head as he opened the creamer.

"Wow, she does that every time. How do you remember how I take my coffee?"

Jake grinned as the young server rolled her eyes. "She's observant." He made eye contact with her. "Ever think about law enforcement, Becca?"

Instead of making a joke, she sighed. "Every day, but Momma would track me down and kill me."

The newcomer nodded. "Your mom's smart. Law enforcement is not an easy job for young, pretty females."

She started smacking gum no one had noticed her chewing earlier. "So are you ready to order so I can get it right out to you, sir?"

"I'll take Minnie's Special but turkey bacon instead of pork, make sure it's very crispy, remove the yellows from the eggs and the toast has to be 100% wheat."

"Sure, anything else?" She sounded bored, but her jaw still attacked the poor gum in her mouth.

"Is your orange juice freshly squeezed?"

"Mother wouldn't serve it if it wasn't." Her eyes tightened.

She reminded him of Vickie, and Ryan didn't even realize he had just made an important enemy.

"Good, then that's all." He crossed his arms and focused on the sheriff. "I want to reassure you that I would be the best candidate to replace you. You could relax and go fishing without worrying about leaving your county in the wrong hands."

Sherriff Johnson leaned forward on his elbows

and crossed his forearms. "Well, that's a mighty nice offer, but I'm not sure I'm ready to retire. Jake and I have worked together for a while now and he…"

"Oh, Jake, I'm willing to work with you. Don't get intimidated by my record. With my experience and masters degree in criminal justice, I can take this county into the twenty-first century. Hey, let's start with the twentieth century first. Am I right?" He laughed at his own joke and slapped Jake on the back.

Giving Ryan a tight smile, Jake cut his gaze to the men sitting around him. No, they were not happy about the thought of Ryan being the county sheriff.

Becca brought out his plate and juice. With a forced smile, she asked if he needed anything else. He waved her off as he told the men more glory stories. Jake looked at his watch.

Vanderbilt kept talking as he cut up his pecan-covered waffles. "J.W., I know your son-in-law, Tommy Miller. He told me you and Dub Childress were the heartbeat of this community. He said if I wanted to run, I'd need your support."

J.W.'s face tightened, and he looked at Ryan with new suspicion. "How do you know Tommy?"

"I met him when he was running for Senate. He's the one that suggested I move to Clear Water. Best move I've ever made. After the big-city life, I love the simplicity of the hill country."

Jake shifted in the booth and the old springs squeaked. He'd had enough. "It's been a good morning, but I've got to go." He stood and pulled out his wallet.

J.W. stopped him. "Don't worry about that. We've got you covered, Jake."

They each threw money on the table.

Sheriff Johnson nodded to the man still eating. "Ryan."

"Hey, are you leaving me to eat alone?"

Dub patted him on the back. "We have to get to work. Not all of us can be retired."

Ryan stood. "But I wanted to talk to you about supporting me for sheriff."

J.W. turned, the only one to answer him. "We'll be up at the church Wednesday night. You can tell us more there. Have a good day."

Jake stood with the three men on the sidewalk. People honked and waved as they drove past. He looked down the main strip. Flags waved outside the storefronts, and the old timers played dominoes in front of the feed store. This was his town.

J.W. spoke first. "Well, son, did that help you?"

Jake grinned. "I'm definitely motivated." The thought of that man as sheriff left a nasty taste in his mouth. "I'm honored that you trust me enough to give me your support."

Shaking hands, Johnson and Dub said goodbye and got in their vehicles.

"Jake, I couldn't be prouder if you were my own

son, and I believe this is the right move for you and our county. I also feel I need to talk to you about Vickie. She's more fragile than she appears," J.W. said.

Jake's nerves tightened again. "I know. She puts up a good front."

"Yeah. I just wanted you to know I supported her divorce, despite everything her mother says. Tommy's failed run for Senate nearly destroyed her. Probably would have been worse if he had managed to win. She gave everything she had to him, and he just walked away from her and the kids. I personally suspect he married her because of the years I was a state representative.

"I wouldn't doubt it. Tommy always had a long-term plan. J.W., I care for Vickie, and Seth and Ashley are great kids." Waiting for J.W.'s response, his muscles tightened, and he stopped breathing. He had always looked up to this man.

J.W. nodded. "You'd be good for her and the kids. But I have to tell you, she'll probably throw a fit when she hears you're running for political office."

He stuffed his fists into the pockets of his jacket and shrugged his shoulders. "It's only for the local sheriff. That's a huge difference from what Tommy was doing."

"I'm just giving you the heads-up. If you do decide to run for sheriff, she might get a bit upset."

"I'm not even sure yet if I want to run. Even if I

did, I'm not Tommy, and I think Vickie would understand the difference."

"Humph, you would think."

With a handshake, they headed to their trucks. He would see Vickie in a couple of days and the thought actually made him happier than three of his heroes asking him to run for sheriff.

# Chapter Eight

The small sliver of the moon gave no light to the empty streets of Clear Water. Jake cruised down Main Street.

He brought the car to a stop in front of the Mercantile. Something was off. His gut told him to go in and investigate, but he couldn't quite find the physical evidence. He put the patrol car in reverse and pulled into the empty parking lot.

Maybe he was overreacting because he knew Vickie was in charge of the store for two weeks and he didn't want anything to happen on her watch.

He called in to the dispatch to let them know he was walking the perimeter. Moving around the side of the building, he heard it. Movement from inside stopped him. It could be a raccoon.

Snickering, followed by an angry shushing sound. Not raccoons. He got in touch with dispatch again and updated the call.

Jake moved to the back door, surprised to find

it not only open but the key still in the lock. A part of him didn't want to go any farther into the building. Gritting his teeth, he knew who he would find.

Easing open the door, Jake paused and listened. Deeper into the store he heard the laughing again and a bottle breaking.

"Cut it out. Now we have to clean up," Seth said in a coarse whisper.

"Don't be such a baby. No one knows we're here. Just leave it."

Jake thought he recognized the voice as Danny Miller, the oldest son of Steve Miller, a cousin of Tommy's.

Jake found the light switch and flipped it on. Like rats caught in the kitchen, four boys scurried around. Mike and James Miller, about the same age as Seth, bumped into each other. Seth knocked over a display of chips, trying to find a place to hide. About that time, the sheriff pulled up with lights on. Danny, the oldest Miller, panicked and tried to run out the front door. Forgetting it was locked, he hit the glass hard and nearly knocked himself out.

"Each of you, get in front of the meat counter."

The boys stopped.

The middle Miller, Mike, started talking fast. "It was Seth's idea. We were mindin' our own business when he called sayin' he had the key. We didn't do anything against the law if we had the key."

Sheriff Johnson came in the back door. "Well, what do we got here?" He looked at the floor where the broken soda bottle had been left. "Some breaking and entering?"

"Seth had the key. We didn't break in," Danny almost yelled.

"Unless he stole the key."

Jake remained silent as he walked over to the candy shelf and picked up a rifle along with a backpack. He laid them on the checkout counter before picking up another backpack that Danny had dropped by the front door. He unloaded both backpacks. They had been stuffed full of drinks, candy and beef jerky.

Jake turned to the boys and stared them in the eye. "You broke into a place of business and stole over a hundred dollars' worth of merchandise while carrying a weapon. Do you understand how much trouble you're in right now?"

"Boys, this is the kind of thing that gets you sent to juvie, over in Uvalde," the sheriff said as he picked up the third backpack.

The three brothers started talking at once. Jake noticed Seth remained silent.

"It was Seth's idea."

"We was just goin' coon huntin'."

"We couldn't leave the gun in the truck. If it had gotten stolen, Dad would have skinned us."

Jake crossed his arms over his chest and raised one eyebrow. The boys all went silent and stared at their feet.

"Does your father know you're out tonight?"

With their heads still down, they mumbled a no.

Jake looked at fifteen-year-old Danny. "This kind of thing will stop you from getting your driver's license. Does your dad know you have his truck?"

"No, sir."

The sheriff gathered the backpacks and rifle. "I'm going to lock these in my trunk. I'll be right back."

Danny Miller's eyes went wide. "My dad will kill me if I don't bring his rifle back."

Jake frowned at him. "You should have thought about that before you stole it." Jake rested a hand on his gun. All the boys' gazes followed the movement. "Now, what we have to find out is if Seth's mother is going to press charges."

The sheriff walked back in and stood next to Jake. Jake turned to him. "Do we take them in?"

Squinting his eyes, Sheriff Johnson looked at each boy. Sweat started to bead on each of their upper lips.

"These three live next to me. I'll take them home and talk with their dad. I'm sure he'll take care of it. You take Seth. I'll interview Victoria in the morning. Then we'll have to see if the Buchannans want to press charges." He put his hands on his hips. "Every one of you will be here 5:30 in the morning to clean up the mess you made and apologize to Ms. Lawson. Do you understand?"

They each nodded their head.

Jake gestured toward the back. "Come on, Seth.

I'm parked on the side of the building." He followed Seth out.

He hated being the one to give Vickie the bad news. Seth had seemed to be doing better. Now he was deeper in angry muck and unscrupulous choices.

They slid into the front of the patrol car and sat in silence for a minute before Jake started the engine. He gripped the steering wheel and shook his head. "You understand how hurt you mother's going to be? You snuck out again and stole from her."

"I didn't take anything. I just wanted to change the marquee outside to send Rachel a secret message." He slumped deeper into the seat and stared out the passenger window. "It was a joke."

"The joke got a little out of hand, didn't it? You like Rachel. So is this your plan to impress Pastor John? You think this is a good way to get him to respect you?

Seth slammed his fist into the side of the door and glared at Jake. "You don't understand! You think I'm just a kid. We like each other, really like each other."

Jake took a deep breath. "Seth, believe it or not, I do understand. I had a special girl about your age. The feelings might be real, but you still have a lot of growing up to do, and this will not make points with her father, who also happens to be your pastor. What about your mother? How can she trust you?"

"If you really cared you wouldn't tell my mom. She'll just get all stressed out again."

"You're right. She is going to get stressed again, but I'm not the one that should tell your mom. You snuck out. You stole from her. You're telling her."

"You don't like me. I talked to my dad yesterday to tell him about the flags I pulled. He said you're just using me to impress Mom." He crossed his arms over his chest and pulled deeper into himself. Turning his head, he went back to staring out the window.

Jake clenched his jaw. He wanted to pound Tommy. His son called him, excited about his success, and Tommy managed to turn it into something ugly.

"Seth, I know what it's like to have your father missing from your life. I understand being angry. But you can't act out this way. It only hurts your mom."

"My father is not missing, and I'm not angry." He sent a quick glare to Jake. "I'm just bored of this stupid town. I'm going to go live with my dad."

With a sigh, Jake stopped trying to talk to Seth. The boy was too angry to listen.

Jake eased his patrol car up Vickie's drive. He scanned the area. He couldn't see much. "What happened to the security light?"

The boy just shrugged, still refusing to speak. He'd have to make Vickie realize how important those lights are to their safety.

"Jake, please just let me slip back in my window. I promise I won't do it again."

He turned off the engine and stared at Seth. The kid looked like he was about to cry. "You say you're in love and it's real. Then as a real man you have to take responsibility for your action and accept the consequences. You stole from your mother and endangered her job and the trust the Buchannans gave her." He unlocked his seat belt and leaned toward Seth. "You're walking into that house, returning the key and apologizing. You will also take any discipline she hands out. Are we clear?"

"Yes, sir," he gritted through his teeth.

Their boots crunched the dry grass as they made their way to the small porch. The outside light came on, and the door opened.

Her heart had accelerated at the sound of a car door slamming, then another. Realizing it was Jake's black-and-white patrol vehicle did nothing to ease her fear.

"Jake? What are you doing here? The headlights scared me. Oh, no." She ran down the wobbly steps. "Seth, what happened? Are you okay?"

"He's fine. Let's step inside."

Her brain, disoriented from sleep, had a hard time processing what stood before her. "Can someone please tell me what is going on?" She pulled the light robe tighter around herself.

With his hand on Vickie's shoulder, Jake herded

her and Seth up the worn steps and into the center of the narrow living room. She glanced to the small hallway. "Seth should be in his bed." Looking back at them, she lowered her voice. "You snuck out again?" Her gaze darted between Seth and Jake, mentally begging them to say something, anything. The silence went on a bit too long, pulling her nerves tighter than a barbed-wire fence.

"Jake, was he with Rachel again?" She locked in on his face. He looked grim but shook his head before making a pointed stare at Seth.

She waited. *Please, God, help me be wise and respond the way You need me to.* "Seth, tell me why you're with Officer Torres."

Seth shuffled a bit then pulled his hand out of his pocket and held out keys. She took them, but they just made her more confused.

With trembling fingers, she rubbed hard against the pain developing between her eyes. She turned to Jake. "I don't understand. Why are you bringing Seth home at two in the morning?" Shifting back to her son, she asked, "And why do you have my store keys? I'm getting a little nervous here, guys."

"Mom, I'm sorry. I didn't mean for them to take anything. I wanted to leave a message for Rachel on the Mercantile marquee. I was going to get the letters in the office, but Danny and his brothers started taking things."

After a heavy silence, Jake added. "They also had a gun on them."

"A gun? You broke into the store, my store with my keys? Seth!" She rubbed the palm of her hand over her brows. "I don't understand. Where did you get a gun? How did you get into town?"

"I didn't have the rifle. It was theirs. I'd been texting Danny. We were bored. There's nothing to do around here."

Jake crossed his arms and flexed his jaw.

Seth looked down on the ground. "I'm sorry, Mom."

"Hand me your phone." She held her hand out, palm up.

"What?"

"You heard me. You said you needed a phone for emergencies to reach me. Since you are grounded, you will be with me or at school."

"That's no fair! What about Dad?"

"Quiet! Your sister's asleep." She stepped closer to him, clenching her teeth. "If you need to talk to your father, you can use my phone."

"Dad hates you! He won't answer your phone. This is all your fault. The divorce, Daddy getting married, everything is your fault because you're too hard to live with!"

Vickie took a deep breath into her lungs then pointed to his door. "Go to bed."

"I'm going to live with Dad."

Vickie bit her lip to stop the words she wouldn't be able to take back. Her son stood before her, rage pouring out of him. She closed her eyes and counted, the way the counselor taught her. Praying for God to take control, she took a couple more deep breaths.

She was hurt but so was her son. The man she really wanted to yell at was in Florida. Vickie opened her eyes.

"Hand me your phone and go to bed. We'll talk about this in the morning." She held out her hand. He gave it to her then without another word he stalked back to his room.

With the slamming of his door, she immediately fell into the small, upholstered chair, face hidden behind her shaking hands. Her own son had stolen from her and broken into the store. "I thought he was doing better. After the game the other day, he seemed happy. Now he's stealing?"

Jake's knee brushed hers as he moved to sit on the sofa. His large hand covered her shoulder. "In the car he told me he had spoken with his father earlier. Tommy told him I was using him to get to you. I'm also guessing he wasn't so proud of Seth's five flags. Victoria, your son is hurt and angry. And it's not at you, not really."

Vickie crossed her arms and started rocking. "That might be true, but I'm the one that has to deal with it." She paused, taking in the dingy colors of her living space. "I don't know what to do."

Jake leaned in closer. "The sheriff told the boys…"

"Sheriff Johnson knows? Oh, he's my dad's friend." She closed her eyes and started rocking again.

"Vickie, I had to call him. He took the Miller boys home. It's okay. He deals with this kind of thing. He told the boys it was up to the Buchannans to press charges. I know Rhody. He will probably work something out with the boys. The sheriff told them to meet you at 5:30 a.m. when you open. They'll clean and do whatever else you need done."

She nodded. "That's good. I can give Seth extra jobs to do at the store to earn back his phone." She looked at Jake. "What do you think?"

He nodded and took her hand in his. "There's also a mentoring program that Pastor John runs. It includes some basic life skills and anger management, communication-type workshops. It's mostly hands-on activities. Some Christian counselors are part of the program, helping others work through any issues in their lives."

"Like the destruction of their family?" She jumped up. Her stomach rolled. It would be so easy to let Jake hold her hand and take care of everything. Pacing the small space, she stopped in front of the family portrait. "I have to find a way to fix this. Tommy's good at illusions. I can rip our wedding pictures apart, but how do I keep my children together? I've been asking God what to do. I still don't know. What's wrong with me?"

"What?" He laughed softly. "Other than being

brutally honest? You do tend to say whatever you're thinking. But overall you're wonderful."

She threw the small pillow from the chair at him. Sending him a weak smile, she moved to the kitchen and started putting up clean dishes.

"I should put bars on his window." After rearranging the items next to the stove, she started to wipe off an already clean countertop.

"Vickie, you can't do that. If a fire started, he'd be trapped. I could help you with some motion sensors. When I come to watch you build your steps, I can install the devices. It's not difficult. My offer for dinner out when we finish still stands."

She started scrubbing the cabinet doors. "This is the reason we can't be together. I'm messed up. My family is broken. Your mother's right. You need someone ready to love you completely and have your own family." Opening a narrow door, she pulled out some more cleaners and sprinkled the sink. "I can't be that woman right now." Her whole body shook with the force of her polishing. "What are Katy and Rhody going to say when they get back?" She turned looking for her phone. "I'll have to call them. What time is it in Hawaii?"

He walked to the edge of the kitchen. "Come here."

She looked up at him. "What?"

"Just come here."

He was so arrogant sometimes, thinking he could tell her what to do. She rinsed the sink out and dried her hands. Looking back at him, she shook her head no.

He opened his arms and waited for her to step into them.

Her need to be held won. With her arms tucked against her chest, she let him pull her into his embrace. They stood in silence, neither moving.

She waited but he didn't say or do anything. She finally asked, "Now what?"

He chuckled softly against her hair. "Nothing. Be still."

She closed her eyes and focused on the sound of his heart. His warmth and scent of leather and Irish soap surrounded her. Calmness eased through her, and for the first time since she came home, the peace she had been seeking settled around her.

Vickie felt like she could stay like this forever. With a sigh, she went deeper into Jake's warmth.

The old clock on the wall clicked the minutes away. In a few hours, she would be taking the kids to her mom's.

She groaned. Her mother wouldn't be taking Seth to school today. Seth needed to go to the store with her. He would have to walk to school from the store.

The store she was in charge of for two weeks. With a deep sigh, she stepped back and stood up straight. "Thank you for everything, Jake. I think it's time for you to go."

He nodded. "I want to talk to you more about the mentoring program. I would love to be Seth's mentor. There's also some family resources for siblings and grandparents." He grinned. "I think your mother might have the hardest time with moving on from the divorce."

She closed her eyes and laughed. "You might be right. She thought Tommy would make a perfect husband. She hates being wrong." She chewed on her bottom lip. She knew she should not invite him or find ways to be around him, but she couldn't stop herself. "What are you doing Saturday?"

"Watching you build new steps."

"Right." She smiled and tucked her hair back. "How long will that take?"

"It should take a few hours. Why?"

"I told the kids I'd take them riding over at the ranch. You could come and tell us more about the mentoring program. I'm taking a picnic lunch with us, but it's not a date." He needed to understand she could not go there with him.

He grinned as he leaned over the counter. "Right." Knocking his knuckles against the countertop he pushed back. "It's not a date. I'll be here."

She couldn't stop herself from grinning back. Okay, they had become grinning fools. She started planning lunch for Saturday.

He stopped at the door. "Is your security light off or burnt out?"

She shrugged, realizing she hadn't even noticed. "I have no idea. Where would I check?"

"I'll check on my way out."

And he was gone. Her trailer seemed bigger without his body filling the space and colder without his warmth. She slid back the curtain and followed his movements to the utility pole. He opened a box and the area became flooded with light. She could only assume Seth had turned it off to sneak around easier.

Jake must have seen her because he waved before folding into his black-and-white. She waved back, leaving her hand on the cold glass as she watched him leave.

# Chapter Nine

"Here's the last board, Mom." The smell of fresh-cut wood filled the air. With Jake's help, Seth had begrudgingly cut the wood for the steps.

She took the two-by-four and laid it straight. Seth handed her a nail. With this step completed, they would have new, safe stairs to the front door.

*They had done it.* Hitting the nail gave her a sense of empowerment. She really liked the feeling. Taking the final nail from Seth, she glanced over at Jake. As promised, he watched from a distance, only helping when needed. She loved the way he ignored Seth's resentment toward him, while still including him. Now he laughed at something Ashley said.

Her daughter had her tongue out concentrating on her own project. Jake had arrived with a kid-sized pink toolbox that included a little metal hammer covered in purple flowers. He said they needed their house number posted by the front gate so it would be easier to find them in case of an emergency.

He was so good with the kids. He held the bottle of water Ashley had given him earlier and now Vickie watched as he arched his neck and took a long drink.

"Ouch!" She dropped her hammer and grabbed her thumb.

"Mom! What happened?" Seth held her arm, concern on his face.

"Nothing. I'm fine." She gave him a lopsided grin. "I wasn't paying attention and hit my thumb."

"You're bleeding." He turned away. "I'll get the first-aid kit."

Jake and Ashley stopped what they were doing to rush to her. He took her hand in his. "What happened?"

She lowered her head. How embarrassing was this? She had just been so proud of herself. Well, pride cometh before a fall.

She pulled her hand out of his warm fingers. "It's nothing, really. I just hit my nail with the hammer. Get it? Ha-ha, my nail."

Jake raised one eyebrow and looked at her as if she'd gone crazy. Seth returned with the red bag. He cut in front of Jake, forcing him to move back. "Mom, was that a joke?"

"Well, since no one laughed I have to guess, no."

"Here, let me wash it off." Her son took charge, opened an antiseptic wipe and went to work.

"You're silly, Mommy." Her daughter curled up against her other side. "Is it bleeding?"

Jake leaned against the post. "You'll want to keep an eye on it. Your nail could turn black and fall off."

Seth looked up with big eyes, apparently his hostility forgotten for a moment. "Really? Cool." Then he looked closer at her thumb. "It has a cut and it's all red." He turned back to Jake. "Should we take her to the doctor?"

Vickie stood up. "I'm fine. Thank you, Seth, for taking care of me." She spread her arms in front of their new steps. "Who wants to drive the last nail and finish our entryway?"

Ashley jumped up and down. "I want to. I want to. I can use my special hammer."

Jake picked up the number post they had been working on and called Seth. "We'll put this on the fence while the girls put the last step together. Okay?"

With a sigh, Seth followed him to the front of their long driveway. Jake turned, walking backward. "Don't forget you promised a tour of the ranch and lunch."

"The last one to the stables has to clean the stalls!" Vickie yelled back. "Come on, Ashley, we'll be there before they even finish."

Jake stood in the saddle, stretching his legs. It had been years since he rode out on trails. The cool air refreshed him. Some of the trees had new growth bravely pushing their way out, giving the hillsides spots of bright green mixed with the live oaks and cedar.

Vickie brought her palomino mare up next to his dark gelding, her knee brushing his. "So it's been a while for you, too?"

"I try roping about once a week, at the fair-grounds, but it's a quick run. How did we used to spend all day on horseback?"

She pointed to the kids up ahead. Ashley's shorter pony trotted to keep up with Seth's old bay. "We were younger and loved being outdoors. Seth's riding Buddy."

Buddy was the giant gelding Jake had ridden years ago when they explored the ranch as kids. He had loved being with her. Thoughts of their past and possible future tangled up his brain as he looked at her now.

She raised her voice, calling out to her children. "Stay on the path."

The cool air brought a bit of color to her cheeks and nose. The smile on her face warmed his heart.

"He must be about thirty now." He chuckled, re-membering how obstinate that horse could be when it came to crossing any water. "He only crossed the water for you."

She laughed. "He'd do anything for me. He loves Seth, too." The plodding of the hooves and the squeak of the leather created a comfortable rhythm as they rode on in silence.

"Jake, thank you for giving the toolbox to Ashley. I didn't even know they had pink and purple hammers and screwdrivers."

"I saw it at Bergmann's Lumberyard while picking up a few things and knew it would keep her busy with her own project while you and Seth built the steps." He ducked under a low-hanging branch. "I thought she might use some girl power, too."

Vickie's laughter sounded sweet on the fresh breeze. "Your mother's right. You need children, a lot of little girls hanging all over you and a few dark-haired boys to get in trouble."

"I have yet to meet a girl that's brave enough to have me." Jake studied her profile. Did he tell her? She'd been the only one he ever imagined being the mother of his children. How long would it take her to run back to the barns?

If she was smart, she'd run. He had nightmares of becoming like his father, but what if he couldn't control his emotions? What if he could be a man like her father, instead? Could he risk her and her children to test his character? "I love my mother, but there're many things she's not right about."

"You, Jake Torres, would make a wonderful father. She is absolutely right about that." She looked off in the opposite direction. Ahead, the kids startled some birds out of the lower bushes. "I…um…have heard you don't date any of the local girls. Rumor has it you haven't had any serious relationships."

He gave her a quick wink. "Been checking up on me, have you?"

"Jake, it's a town of four hundred people. Everyone knew I was divorced before the papers had been filed. They love telling me all they know about you."

He shrugged and looked down. "There were a couple of girls while I was enlisted, but it never felt right." He pulled up on the reins and waited for her to stop next to him, making sure he had firm eye contact. "None of them compared to you."

For a moment, silence filled the space between them. Only the birds made a sound. Vickie's hand went to the base of her neck as she whispered, "Oh, Jake."

"Victoria, do you think it's too late for us?" He leaned forward until inches separated them. "We were good friends. Do you think we could try that again?"

"Jake." She choked on his name.

His dark eyes held her and he smiled. "Vickie."

She shook her head. "I'm a mess. Not just my marriage but—" her gaze went up the trail to her children "—my whole life. I have to find a way to be a better person. A whole person, not my mother's image, not Tommy's… I need to…" She sat up straight in her saddle, pulling away from him. "I need to be strong on my own."

Jake reached across the space between their horses and touched her arm, trying to bring her back to him. "I know you. The little girl that nurtured abandoned lambs behind her mother's back.

I remember the Vickie that ran wild on this ranch, jumping from the high rope and climbing to the top of the ridge, dragging me along. She embraced every day with gusto and taught me so much about life. I know her." He needed her to understand. "I know you."

Eyes closed as she swayed. "I lost that girl so long ago. You're going to have to give me time, Jake. I can't trust myself to be your friend right now." She looked back at him and shook her head.

He sat straighter in the saddle, giving her space. "The real you is still in there. You just need to get through all the voices. In the last week, I've seen her. When you're ready, I'll be waiting. I've waited this long." He grinned. "We could start with a simple date. Next weekend is Music Under the Stars in Kerrville. Want to go with me? The kids would have fun."

Her eyes shone with a layer of unshed tears. He flexed his jaw, hating to see her cry.

"Jake, you make it so easy to say yes, but I can't risk my kids. Seth's so far from healing and I, well, I don't have a whole heart to give you."

She stayed focused on his face; he gave her points for courage, but he didn't like what she said. He broke eye contact and looked for the kids.

Her voice grew stronger. "It wouldn't be fair to Seth or you. Once I work everything out, maybe." She shrugged. "But not now."

He risked a glance at her. Sighing, she turned

her face away. "The kids are getting too far ahead."
With a kick, she took off. One look over her shoulder and he caught a glimpse of the Vickie he knew and loved.

"Race you!" she challenged him.

Stunned for a moment, Jake sat there, and then he grinned. Okay, so he'd take that as a maybe. He knew it was for the best. Being around her just gave him false hope that he could be a better man than his father. Something he didn't really want to test.

With a flick of the leather reins, he urged his horse forward and followed her around the bend.

As he came up next to her, the tree-lined path opened to a clearing with the river running along the edge. Sixty-foot cypress trees twisted their roots along the banks and rocks refusing to give up, come flood or drought. He wanted roots like that with Vickie. A mix of native trees created a semicircle around the small, grassy meadow.

Seth turned in his saddle and looked at them. "Mom, is this it?"

She simply answered with a smile and nod. They unpacked their lunch and spread out the thick blanket Vickie had tied to the back of her saddle. They both told the kids stories about the ranch as they ate the chips and chicken wraps.

After a few cookies, the kids left the blanket to explore the area. Seth grabbed a handful of small rocks and stood on the river's edge, skipping them. Jake smiled as he watched the boy patiently show his sister how to hold the rock. He missed having his sister around. "You have good kids, Vickie."

"Thanks. I love them so much. I'm worried about Seth, though. Do you think the mentoring program will help?" She sat cross-legged on the opposite side of the purple throw.

"It'll give him people to talk to if he needs it. Right now, he's confused. Caught between wanting his dad here and hating him for what he's done. That's a tough place for a young boy to be." He watched Seth throw a few rocks, causing them to jump over the water's surface. "The program can help him work through that kind of turmoil. Teach him to rely on God."

She stretched onto her stomach and rested her chin on the palms of her hands. "I could work on that myself. I like being in control, and life has pretty much proved that control is an illusion."

He was on his side, resting on one elbow. He picked at the fresh raspberries, tossing one in his mouth. "So how about going to the Music Festival with me next weekend?"

Laughing, she grabbed a few berries for herself. "Are you trying to make up for the dances you missed?"

"I'm the one who got stood up, so *you*—" he threw a blade of grass at her "—owe *me*."

Flipping over onto her back, she gave the kids a quick glance before studying the clouds.

He scooted down, closer to her. With his hand tucked under his head he stared at the sky, too.

Vickie took a moment to absorb this perfect place in time. The kids laughing in the background. The smells of raspberries and fresh grass. The clouds floating by, changing forms as they moved across the blue sky.

"We used to spend hours discussing everything." Being next to him, just listening to his breathing brought back so many memories. "I guess I was doing all the talking. There's so much you didn't tell me."

A deep chuckle came from his side of the blanket. "Your life was way more interesting. Between your sisters, mother and friends at school, you needed someone to talk to."

Silence hung in the air. When she needed to talk to him the most, she had been shocked to find him gone. "I was devastated when you left the Monday after graduation without a word. I thought you were going to the junior college in Uvalde." She watched a cloud form a heart then slowly come apart. "I had our summer all planned: swimming, dancing at Garner and hanging out. You were just gone." She turned her head to look at him. "You didn't even say anything about enlisting."

"After prom, I didn't see the point in sticking around to watch you and Tommy together."

"What? I never picked Tommy over you. You're the one that disappeared."

"I had to work for a living. You and Tommy had project graduation. You traveled to San Antonio for that leadership thing. You were always doing something as 4-H officers or with student council. You were going to Baylor together."

"I went to Baylor because that's where my parents went. Not because of Tommy." With a deep sigh, she flopped back. "I kept thinking once we got out of high school, Momma couldn't tell me what to do." She wanted to get lost in the sky, in the dreams she'd had as a girl. "Momma loved that Tommy and I went to school together and you left town."

"Your mother made it clear she had big plans for you and that I would drag you down. She might have been right."

She couldn't defend her mother because it was true, so she looked for something else to talk about. Ironically, Tommy had been the one to destroy her dreams.

The kids climbed the giant cypress, the roots exposed with the low water flow. Giant limbs hung out over the river; a thick rope with knots dangled above the water.

Seth yelled at them. "Mom, can we swing?"

Vickie sat up. "No. It's cold, and the river's too low. You just recovered from a head injury. I'm afraid you'll hit the rocks."

"I'm fine. I want to swing without jumping! Come on, Mom, please?"

Ashley tried another tactic. "Mommy, did you swing on it when you were a little girl?"

Jake chuckled and yelled back. "Your mom's the one who taught me to jump."

She glared at him. "You're not helping."

Seth saw the crack and suddenly Jake became an ally. He chiseled at his mother some more. "Come on, Mom! You got to do it! I'll be careful. How about I just swing on the rope? No jumping."

Jake stood up and dusted dried grass off his jeans. "I'll stand close by. The 'V' in the tree makes for a good landing place."

She sighed in defeat. "Okay, but be careful. It wasn't that long ago, I almost lost you."

"That was different, Mom. It was dark, and I jumped in without looking." He turned to Jake. "I don't need your help."

"That's fine, but I'll be here, anyway. Make sure your feet are on the knot."

While the horses grazed, Vickie watched Jake guide her son back to the platform and help him swing out. It seemed each time Seth got a little braver and swung out farther.

All the lost dreams flooded her mind. Her eyes burned. Maybe she couldn't go back, but she could make new memories.

She moved to stand next to Ashley, pulling her daughter close to her, taking in the fast heartbeat and the clean smell of her soap. These two were her treasures, and their father didn't see it. Jake did.

How could she have been so blind? Kissing the top of Ashley's head, she moved away from her.

Gathering the food and blankets, she started humming. Maybe she should go on a real date with Jake Torres. She wanted a new life; maybe he was part of it.

Ashley's sweet laughter joined the soft sounds of nature. Jake had picked her up and swung her high over his shoulder as Seth climbed down from the tree.

As soon as they could find some alone time, she would tell him. It felt right. Blood rushed to her heart. It looked like she was going on her first date with Jake Torres. She could only imagine the look on his face when she announced she had changed her mind.

## Chapter Ten

The kids chatted all the way back to the barns. As they approached the wide corridor of the stables, Rey, the stable's manager, met them, helping Ashley dismount. The old horseman crossed-tied the pony then turned to Seth's big gelding.

Jake followed Vickie as she rode farther into the dim coolness of the stables. Pulling up on the reins, Jake stopped next to the indoor arena. With one swing of his leg, he was out of the saddle. Laying the lead over the nearest rail, he watched Vickie and her mare. He stood a few feet away, one eyebrow up and a smirk on his too handsome face.

She glared at his smile. "What are you laughing at?"

He shrugged his shoulders as he made himself comfortable against one of the huge metal columns, with his arms crossed. "Nothing. Are you going to sit up there all day?"

Her back straight, she looked down at him. "If I want to."

With the help of Rey, Ashley led her pony to his stall. "Mommy, why are you still on Charm?"

Jake answered. "She's thinking of taking her through her paces in the arena."

Seth moved toward them with the big bay following him like a puppy. "We rubbed them down already. Can we go up to the house?"

Vickie nodded. "I'll come get you when I'm ready to go home."

Once their horses had hay and were settled into their stalls, the kids ran off. Rey stepped out from the tack room with a couple of halters. "Do you need anything else, Ms. Vickie?"

"No, no, I'm good. Thanks for helping the kids."

Jake remained silent until the manager had left. "Okay, now tell me the truth. You can't move your legs, can you?"

Her back stiffened as she looked up to the rafters of the covered area. "It has been a long time since I've ridden."

He made his way to her left side. "Do you need some help?"

The leather reins became entwined with her fingers as she fidgeted with them. She stood in the stirrups then went back down. "My hamstrings are cramping, and my legs are totally numb. I think if I tried to stand, I would make a puddle on the ground." A shift in the saddle caused her muscles to bunch and flex. "This is so embarrassing."

"Stretch your legs then I'll help you down."

She fixed her eyesight straight ahead, her muscles tightening as she pressed all her weight into the stirrup.

"Come on, I've got you." Charm nudged his shoulder and flipped her tail.

A sweet giggle escaped from Vickie. The sound lightened Jake's mood, making him want to laugh. Today had been perfect. Maybe here in the barn he could convince her they made a perfect match.

With a heavy sigh, she leaned slightly forward, bracing herself on the saddle horn as she swung her right leg over the horse. For a minute, her knee rested on the back of the saddle. She groaned. "I'm stuck. I can't lift it any higher."

Jake made sure not to laugh. He knew Vickie's pride couldn't handle that right now. Reaching up, he guided her ankle all the way over. Moving his hands over her leather belt, he held her in place for a moment, using his body to support her.

"Can you slide to the ground?" he whispered, not wanting to break the fragile bond between them. If she felt challenged or trapped she'd run and he would lose this opportunity to have a real discussion about their future.

A slight nod, and she eased down to the brick-covered ground. Knuckles gripping the edge of the saddle, she leaned her forehead against the suede seat. "I am so out of shape. I don't remember riding being so hard on the legs." She dropped her hands and twisted around. Her eyes twinkled as she smiled up at him. "Thanks."

He brought his arms up and gripped the edges of the saddle, still warm from her touch.

"Anytime." He smiled.

She leaned in and tilted her head up and whispered close to his ear, "About this weekend, do you still want to go?" She paused, her breath soft and sweet. "With me?"

He pulled back, wanting to makes sure he heard right, but the smell of fresh lavender called him to move closer. He needed to move slowly.

*Don't rush her, Torres.* She wanted to go to Kerrville with him. *Resist the urge to kiss her.*

Her arms encased his ribs. Her heart beat heavy against his chest as he held his breath, waiting to get back in control of his emotions. His gaze slipped to her full lips. Mistake. The kiss he had dreamt about was within reach.

"Jake! Vickie!" Her father's voice split them apart like lightning.

Vickie turned her back to him and started undoing the girth on the saddle. He didn't even have time to mourn the loss of her warmth before J.W. stomped down the corridor. "The kids said you were riding in the arena."

Vickie heaved the saddle and blanket off the mare's back. "We finished."

Jake stepped in front of her and took the burden from her arms. "For now, anyway." He winked at her glare. Nothing could kill his mood now, even an untimely interruption by her father. He smiled. Yes, she could take all the time she needed.

She turned from him to her father. "What do you need, Daddy?"

Walking into the tack room their voices faded as he deposited the saddle on the rack and looked for the brushes. Caddy of brushes in hand, he headed back to the horses. He needed to unsaddle his mount and brush him down. Maybe next time he could haul his geldings over and they could explore other areas of the ranch.

Stepping out of the dark room, Vickie met him with the saddle from his horse. "Daddy said he was looking for you." She raised her eyebrows in question. He shrugged back. He took the saddle and handed the caddy with the brushes to her. "I'll be right there."

Less than a minute later, he joined them by the horses. "Did you need something from me?" he asked as he started checking the sorrel's hooves.

Jackson chuckled as he patted the horse's neck. "For you to tell me if you're ready to run for sheriff."

Vickie gasped. "Sheriff?"

Jake had a bad feeling this wasn't going to go well. He pinched the bridge of his nose and rubbed.

"You didn't tell her?" J.W. shifted a quick glance

from Jake to Vickie. "I got the impression you planned to tell her when you fixed the steps."

She jabbed her chest. "*I* built the stairs, and no, he didn't tell me he decided to become a politician." The softness of her eyes disappeared as she glared at Jake.

J.W. started backpedaling. "It's just a local office. He hasn't even decided yet. You have to agree, sweetheart, he'd make a great county sheriff."

Jake watched as her jaw tightened. She was not happy.

"You're right, Daddy. Jake would make a perfect sheriff."

J.W shot him an "I told you so" look. "Yeah, well, the deadline to add your name is getting close, and I know you have to make a decision about your state job." He patted Jake on the shoulder. "We really need to know this next week. Vickie, your mother is making plans with the kids for dinner tonight. Jake, why don't you join us?"

Vickie shot him a glare that dared him to say yes. "Sorry, but I'm on patrol tonight."

J.W. nodded. "Another time, then? Vickie, I'll see you up at the house in a bit?"

"Tell Mom I'll be there as soon as I finish with the horses."

Jake watched J.W. exit the stables. Taking a deep breath, he turned back to Vickie, knowing he needed to find a way to calm the brewing storm.

# Chapter Eleven

Every muscle vibrated with betrayal as she finished brushing Charm's coat. "So Daddy's backing you for sheriff. Congratulations." She turned her back and started braiding the mare's tail. "Tommy never got his endorsement, one of the many things that destroyed my marriage."

"Vickie, growing up I never even dreamed being sheriff was possible." He had his hands in his pockets. "Without your dad, I still wouldn't consider myself a candidate."

She threw the brush into the caddy. How could she be such an idiot? She was tired of being used.

She would have thought she had learned her lesson with Tommy. "So that's what this has been all about, getting Daddy's support?"

"What are you talking about?" He stepped closer to her.

She moved to the other side of her mare and focused on the end of the braid. Her hands started to shake. "Asking me out. Helping Seth. Bringing Ashley gifts."

"Are you serious?" He leaned across the back of her mare as he glared at her. His eyebrows wrinkled from his frown.

"Hey, Tommy even married me to get Daddy's funding. Was that your next move?" She wrapped the hair tie at the end of the braid. She took a chance and glanced up at him.

His eyes narrowed as he pressed his beautiful lips in a tight line. "You are really messed up." He moved back, stepping away from her.

Fine. The farther away he got from her, the better. She bit the inside of her cheek and ran her hand down Charm's back leg. Cupping the hoof, Vickie focused on the horse before talking again. "Tommy ruined us in his losing run for office. I'm sorry, Jake. I can't get involved with another man who needs power over everything."

Looking up, Vickie had never seen such anger in Jake's face. Placing the hoof back down, she leaned into her mare's warmth, needing a friend's support.

He took a step toward her. "I'm not Tommy." Each word clearly pronounced.

"How would I know? You don't tell me anything."

"I wasn't hiding it from you. I just didn't talk about it. You made it clear we're not in a relationship."

"But you said that's where you wanted to go.

You're the one that asked me out several times. Today I was going to say yes, but it's obvious that was a mistake. That's all I ever do, trust the wrong man. I can't trust you."

"Trust me! You can't trust *me?*"

She waved her hands in the air before pointing to his chest. "You left me. You signed up for the marines and left without saying a word." She thrust her chin into the air and gritted her teeth. She would not cry in front of him.

He hooted. "Yeah, let's bring up what we did twelve years ago."

She leaned forward and pointed at her chest each word intense. "I waited for you."

"You waited for me?" Sarcasm dripped like honey. "I was the one under the bridge while you danced with Tommy. You made plans to go to Baylor with Tommy. Yeah, I left. And when I called home all I heard about was you and Tommy." He held his hand up and started counting off the digits. "By February you were engaged, June you were married, by September you had dropped out of school and in March you had Seth. Sorry if I didn't realize you were waiting for me."

The vastness of her mistake overwhelmed her for a moment. Her lungs froze; air was impossible to find. She had waited. She had allowed her mother to push her and guide her toward Tommy.

Too impatient to wait on God's plan, she rushed ahead with her own. She was horrified to see it through Jake's eyes, but she *had* waited all summer and into the fall. She hadn't said yes to Tommy until after Christmas. "Eight months. I waited eight long months without a single word from you. To a eighteen-year-old girl, that's a lifetime."

By Christmas, Tommy had worn her down and she had given up on Jake. Her mom had convinced her she didn't want to be a soldier's wife. She rubbed her head. The pounding made it hard to organize her thoughts.

"Well, I'm the big loser because Tommy didn't want *me*. He wanted Daddy's money and backing to run for political office and the perfect family portrait for the campaign. I'm not going there again."

"I never even thought I could be sheriff until your father asked me. I respect him and I wouldn't take anything I don't deserve. For you to compare me to Tommy shows how little you know me." He turned and headed to the barn doors.

"You can't go. I'm not finished. I wrote you letters, left messages with your mom to have you call me. Not a single word from you, not one." He didn't even look back. She yelled louder, not caring who heard. "Your mom didn't want us together, either. This is *not* all my fault. Jake Torres, come back here!" He kept walking. "Jake!"

He didn't say a word. He didn't slow down, not one backward glance as he disappeared through the huge doorway.

Fine, let him leave. He was good at that. She

didn't need him, anyway. Brushing Charm's neck, she fought the urge to hit something. The mare turned her head and bumped Vickie's shoulder with her velvet-soft muzzle.

"Charm, I feel like I just failed a test." She rested her head on the horse's forelock and rubbed her jaw. "God, I know I'm struggling with following Your will. I need Your strength. What should I do?" She wrapped her arm around Charm's neck and cried.

# *Chapter Twelve*

Vickie stared at the soft, yellow material in her hand. It would be beautiful on Maggie's dark skin. She shook her head and smiled. God had a strange way of working.

Just a few months ago, she had told Lorrie Ann to stay away from Pastor John. She had done everything in her power to chase her out of town. Now she was making the dresses for their wedding. Some might say they were even friends now.

Glancing out the window, she saw the fire pit. Jake deserved the biggest apology. As soon as he pulled up, she planned to start over again, taking full responsibility for her choices and mistakes.

If she wanted Seth to behave that way, she needed to start with herself. Yesterday she allowed all the old fears and anger to color her thoughts and words. Instead of listening to Jake, she lashed out.

She started chewing on her bottom lip. She actually compared him to Tommy. All her ex-husband had cared about was being the big man in the room. His ego needed constant feeding.

She looked back at the pattern and began modifying it for Maggie's curves.

Jake thought of others first. He didn't expect anything in return, not even praise. He just did what was right because it was right.

Seth walked over to the table. "Mom, I'm finished with the dishes. Can I go to my room and play my Xbox while I wait for Jake?"

Vickie looked up from the long swaths of material. "Sure."

As soon as Jake arrived to take Seth to the football game, she'd tell him how wrong she was and that he was right.

Smiling, she started cutting. That should shock him. He would enjoy hearing those words from her since she never said them before.

Jake would forgive her; he always did. Maybe she'd meet him outside and they would actually get that kiss that eluded them twice now.

A car came into her drive. Her heart rate picked up, and she dashed through the living room. Quietly opening the door, she slipped through and closed it just as softly. Her smile couldn't be restrained; one hand on their new railing, she looked up.

The smile vanished. Her mind didn't want to process who sat in her driveway.

Tommy?

A new, sleek Mercedes-Benz was parked next to

her car. With the top down, she could see the grin on his face. Getting out of his vehicle, he started walking toward her with the most outrageous bouquet of roses and orchids she'd ever seen. His perfect blond hair seemed to have thinned since she last saw him.

"Vic! Surprise!" Standing at the bottom of the steps, he offered her the flowers.

She refused to take the offering. "Tommy? What are you doing here?"

"Oh Vic, relax, you're causing deep wrinkles in your forehead." He forced the flowers on her. "These are for you. Two dozen roses, one for each month I was wrong for letting you leave, Vickie."

She had nothing to say. Her brain stopped working. Silence stretched out between them.

"I'm back, babe." His grin covered his whole face. He took one step closer to her. "I realize what a blunder I made, and the orchids are my promise for a better future."

She stared at him, confused. He shouldn't be here. She looked down the empty drive. Where was Jake? Swallowing, she set the vase on the railing and looked back at Tommy. "I thought you were getting married? Where's Jenny?"

His smile dropped. "Oh, she didn't really love me, not like you do. It was a good thing I discovered the truth before I made a huge, huge mistake."

He gave her his sad puppy face, the one that

used to work on her. She sighed. Why did he have to show up now?

"Vic, she just wanted the lifestyle I could give her."

"Lifestyle?" She glanced at the new convertible. "I thought you were broke."

"That's the great news." He reached up and took her hand, pulling her down the steps, closer to him. "Business is great. I've got this big condo project that people are lined up to buy." He pulled her into his arms. "I missed you and the kids so much. I thought getting married again would fix my loneliness."

She pushed against his chest. "Tommy, you could have called or…"

He placed his finger on her lips. Numb, she felt numb from her brain to her toes, or maybe it was the other way around. She had been so ready to move on, to start over with Jake.

Nausea rolled in the pit of her stomach. She wanted to cry. She didn't want to deal with Tommy or his manipulations.

"I realized I was just trying to substitute you and the kids with Jenny. I can't replace you. You're my life. I never appreciated all you did for me." He dropped his arm and stepped back. "Losing that Senate race messed me up. It was hard to come back from that loss. I made colossal blunders. You and the kids should have been my anchor. Instead, I cut and ran from you."

"Tommy, we had problems before the race. I can't forget all the other women." She waved to the flowers. "This is all nice, but you can't just expect us to…" Jake's black truck came down her drive. Both of them watched as he pulled in behind Tommy's Mercedes-Benz. The truck looked as if it could eat the sleek, little car.

An angry sigh came from Tommy. "What's he doing here?"

"He's mentoring Seth, and they have a flag football game today." She bit back a smile and some of the stress left. Why did she feel rescued?

Jake got out and moved toward them. Vickie couldn't help but notice the difference between the two men. In his old marine T-shirt and sweatpants, Jake moved with purpose and power. Even though he was slightly shorter than Tommy, he had twice as much presence. She glanced at Tommy in his pressed suit.

Tommy stepped forward with his hand out. "Torres." The men shook hands. "So you're back in this nowhere town. Army kicked ya out?"

Jake's jaw flexed. "Marines. What brought you to our neck of the woods?"

"My family. Me and Vic here are talking about remarrying."

She gasped. In response to that outlandish comment, her brain short-circuited. There was no way Jake could believe that. But she had been staring at Jake and caught a flash in his eyes and a twitch of his lips. She turned her glare to Tommy.

"I never…"

Jake cut her off. "Congratulations. Where is Seth? Is he ready?"

Tommy took a step closer to Jake. "Seth told me how you're using him to move in on my girl." He laughed as if he had made a joke.

Teeth gritted, Jake stood taller. "She's not your girl anymore."

Her ex threw out his practiced smile. "She's the mother of my children, so she'll always be mine."

Jake moved in closer to Tommy, his jaw taunt and fists tightened.

Tommy took a step back. "Seth is my son, and I'm here to make it right with *my* family. Got a problem with that, Torres?"

Rage exploded in Vickie's veins. Stepping in between them, she pushed on Jake's chest, not daring to touch Tommy. "That's enough. This is not the place."

"You're right." Jake forced himself to relax and moved back. "I'm sorry, Vickie." He shot one last look at her before he turned and strode to his truck. He needed to leave before he hit Tommy, before he did something he'd regret.

As he reached for the handle of his truck, Vickie had her hand on his upper arm.

"Jake, please don't leave like this. Tommy just

showed up. I didn't…" Her eyes became larger each time she blinked. "Oh, Jake, I'm so sorry about yesterday. I…"

"Vickie, I understand. I do." He had to cut her off. "Yesterday is over, and I don't want to hear any apologies about Tommy." He closed his eyes and ran his fingers through his hair. "I want you to be happy." He looked toward the gate. "I can't just stand by and watch."

"But Jake, I need to tell you how sorry…"

Tommy walked up and cut her off. With one arm around her waist, he pulled her close to him.

"Hey, Jake, I owe you an apology. I was out of line back there. I understand what I lost, and hopefully they'll give me another chance to prove I've learned my lesson. I can be the kind of husband and father my family needs." He looked at Vickie and gave her a kiss on the side of her forehead.

Vickie's gaze stayed locked on Jake. She tried to move away from Tommy's grip. She needed Jake to understand. Her kids were in the house. She didn't know what to do. "Jake, I…"

Tommy interrupted her again. "I was a fool to think I could find anything better."

Jake had not made eye contact with her once.

"You're a lucky man, Tommy. Take care of them." Jake jerked open his truck door and slid inside. "Be happy, Vickie."

She stepped forward with more force, breaking the hold Tommy had on her. "But Jake…"

# Chapter Thirteen

Jake slammed his door. He couldn't listen to another word. Twisting the key and with his arm over the seat, he looked behind him. Foot on the gas, he backed out of the drive as fast as he could, out of Vickie's life.

Once outside the gate, he shifted gears and put the truck in Park. He needed a moment to collect his thoughts. The football lay in the seat next to him.

He couldn't continue playing house with Tommy's family. It was time to move on and give up the fantasy of being Vickie's man.

Looking for blessings in this mess, today he could put one of his greatest fears to rest. He had been in a jealous rage seeing Tommy standing next to Vickie, as if he owned her, and not only was Tommy still alive, he hadn't even knocked him flat in the dirt.

*Thank You, God, for helping me hold my temper.*

The knot in his gut relaxed. The rage bouncing around his blood didn't control him. He had stood there with Tommy's arm around Vickie and had walked away. So maybe he wasn't his father.

Reaching for his wallet, he pulled out the blue paper his mother had given him. He had to do this now, before he got weak again. He needed to move forward. With the quick movement of his thumb, he called Anjelica.

While the phone rang, sweat broke out on his upper lip. Why did it feel like he was cheating on Vickie? Maybe he should forget it and hang up.

"Hello?" The soft voice stopped him.

"Anjelica, it's Jake, Jake Torres. My mother gave me your number." He rolled his eyes. How lame was that. A soft laugh didn't make him feel any better.

"I'm so sorry, Jake. Our mothers seem to be plotting our futures according to their wishes."

"Yeah. But that aside, I would like to take you out. I was thinking of going to Music Under the Stars next weekend in Kerrville. We could go together if you're interested."

"I love that festival. Yes, that sounds nice. Thanks for inviting me."

"Okay. Good. I'll pick you up at your house Saturday night around 7 o'clock?"

"I'll see you then. I look forward to it. Thank you."

"Sure. Bye." Jake disconnected the call and sat

there looking at the landscape. He swallowed, trying to relieve the dryness of his throat. Something was in his eye; rubbing it didn't seem to help. With a few hard blinks, he tried to focus on the ranch land surrounding him.

The drought had taken a toll on the land. The normally green hills had a taint of dry brown thread running through them. Maybe his drought was over. Releasing the brake, he drove away from Vickie's house, making sure not to look in the rearview mirror.

Vickie wrapped her arms around her waist, wishing that Jake stood next to her. Instead, her heart ran after the black truck. Tommy moved closer to her, putting his hand on the small of her back.

"He was always jealous of me. Wanted everything I had."

"I think it was the other way around, Tommy."

"What!" Anger flared in his eyes. "So that's how it is now. I make one mistake, and you let Torres come in and take what's mine. I'm here asking for forgiveness."

She had nothing to say. She could see it now. Tommy had to work so hard to gain the popularity that came naturally to Jake. Tommy had made sure everyone knew he was the quarterback that got the team to State. He made jokes at Jake's expense.

Jake always smiled and took it. Jake had been the real team leader, the one everyone looked to for advice and strength. He cared about people and treated them with respect. Tommy used people. How could she let him back into her life?

"It was more than one mistake, more than one affair. I have forgiven you, but that doesn't mean I have to let you back in my life."

"You can't keep me away from my children." He looked at her house. "I can't believe your parents are making my kids live here in this old dump."

"They're not. I wanted to stay here while I saved enough to buy our own place."

"Don't be ridiculous. I have rented the Warren's vacation place up Highway 84. It's a two story, right on the river. You and the kids can move in with me."

"We aren't married anymore, Tommy. I'm not moving in with you."

"Vickie, we were married for almost ten years. We can go down to the courthouse and fix this."

"We are past fixing it. I am not marrying you again. *You* said that I made you so miserable it was my fault you had so many affairs. Why would you want me back? No, Tommy."

"Vic, I know it was my fault now. We have to think about the kids. The faster we get back to normal, the better for them."

"I am thinking of them, Tommy. You broke your vows to me and to your children. They didn't mean anything to you for the last three years. You're the one that ended it. I fought for our marriage, Tommy.

I gave you second and third chances, but you had more important things to do. Now you just want to waltz back into our lives like nothing happened." She turned and stared him in the eye. "No! You have to earn your spot back into their lives. I would be just as happy if you went back to Florida."

"You don't mean that. Think about the kids. I want to be a good father. I want a chance to prove to you that I can be a good husband. I've changed."

The front door opened. "Mom, I thought I heard Jake's truck. What's taking…Dad?" Seth's voice dropped to a whisper.

"Son!" Tommy headed to the steps.

Vickie's heart broke when she saw Seth run to meet his dad. Wrapping his lanky arms around Tommy's chest, Seth had his eyes closed tight.

She could handle Tommy because she knew what to expect, but seeing the hope in Seth's face made her want to grab him and run. Run so far Tommy would never hurt him again. She pressed her thumbs into her eyes. She would not cry in front of Tommy, not with Seth watching. She thought of the scripture she prayed with this morning. *John 14:27. "Do not let your hearts be troubled and do not be afraid."*

*She could do this. God, please guide me to be wise and fearless in Your word.*

"I knew you'd come. Grandma said you'd come back for us."

"Son, I'm so sorry, and I'm here to stay. I've got

a place over on the river, right outside of town. We can be a family."

"Tommy, don't start that now."

Tommy pulled Seth against his side and rolled his eyes. "Moms, what do we do with them? She thinks I need to go back to Florida."

Seth turned on her. "Mom! No."

Tommy patted his son on the back. "Don't worry, she can't chase me off that easy. I've decided not to marry Jenny, and I want us all back together as a family. Give your mom some time. We'll get her on our side."

"Tommy, please." At this point anything she would say he would turn against her.

He smiled at her and shrugged his shoulders before turning back to Seth. "So Jake just left, but he told me something about a flag football game?"

"Mom! You let him leave without me?"

"Hey, no worries, little guy. Not your mom's fault this time. He thought I should take you. You know the father-and-son thing. Sounds like fun. Want to go with your old man?"

Vickie bit her lip. Tommy was already manipulating the truth to get what he wanted. Seth stepped back from his father. "I..." He looked down. "I play..."

"Speak up, son. I can't hear you, and you're staring at the ground. Look me in the eye."

"I play on the line now. I don't play quarterback."

"Well, I'm here now, so we'll get that all straightened out. They're probably jealous. Jake was always stuck on the line."

"I like the line, Dad."

"Nonsense. No one likes the line. That's just where they put the big dumb ones with no talent."

"Tommy, that's enough! Seth has been doing a great job and has sacked the quarterback a number of times."

"They must have a lame quarterback." He wrapped his arm around Seth's shoulders. "Your dad will show them how to play."

Ashley came to the door. Seeing her father, she squealed and ran to him. With both arms around the children, he sent Vickie his best politician smile. He had won. Dread descended over her. If he had changed, that would be great for Seth and Ashley. But what if he hadn't?

Children thrive with two parents in their lives. What if one of those parents was toxic? What would happen to her kids when Tommy returned to his narcissistic behavior? She closed her eyes and asked for God's wisdom.

## Chapter Fourteen

Three hours into the Kerrville music festival, and Vickie had been ready to go home two and half hours ago. Letting the kids convince her to come with Tommy had been a mistake. At least Seth was enjoying himself.

A trail of white lights and colorful flags ran from tree to tree creating a fanciful ceiling with the night sky overhead. People sitting on the long, wood tables tapped their feet to the live music. Others packed the dance floor spinning to the fast-paced fiddle. Ashley had danced herself to exhaustion.

Tonight she could have been here with Jake. Thinking of the man who had been the first to invite her here made her heart hurt. Tommy was not making it easy. He told the same self-important stories repeatedly.

Ashley now slept on her father's shoulder. Her new pink cowboy boots dangled as he held her on one arm. He had been showering the kids with gifts for the last week. She had to give him credit; as a father he'd been more attentive the last six days than he had been at any time during their marriage.

Vickie hinted to Tommy that she wanted to go home, but he seemed determined to stay all night. He was trying to prove something, but she hadn't figured it out yet.

A blonde woman that seemed vaguely familiar stood next to Vickie. "What a precious picture of father and daughter. You must be so happy to have him back."

Not having anything nice to say, she smiled and nodded. With a sigh, she scanned the crowd again. The long, wood tables were covered in red-checkered vinyl. Mason jars and plastic cups cluttered the surface.

She hadn't wanted to come with Tommy, he had the kids beg her. Why was she so weak sometimes? Tommy had a way of making her do things she didn't want to do.

To make her mood worse, everyone that came through the Mercantile made sure she heard the latest rumor. Jake had asked Anjelica to the music festival.

She didn't have time to juggle Jake and her children. With Tommy, she had to stay on guard. Scanning the crowd again, she put her hands in her pockets. Maybe it had just been a rumor to stir her up. She hadn't seen Jake or Anjelica.

He did seem to move a bit fast after not dating

anyone for the last few years. Her mother had a great time fawning over Tommy and pointing out the fact that Jake was dating someone else.

Seth ran up to his father, face flushed and hair sweaty despite the cool nip in the air. "Dad, can I have some more money? The guys want to play the games and buy some food."

"Sure, buddy." Tommy turned to her. "Hey Vic. Can you get my wallet? I can't reach it with Ashley's dead weight."

"Do you want me to take her?"

"No, I don't want to give her up." He looked at the man next to him and pushed blond strands from Ashley's face. "Easy to take 'em for granted until they're taken from you."

No one had taken his children from him. Vickie bit her lip to stop the words. She took a deep sigh and handed him the wallet. He leaned into her and went for a kiss. She turned her head so that it landed on her cheek.

"Oh, come on, Vic. One kiss. I've been a good boy and played by your rules."

She narrowed her eyes and lowered her voice so Seth wouldn't hear. "Tommy, this is not a game, and there is no kissing."

She went to pull out a ten, but Tommy stopped her.

"Give him the fifty. The boy has friends to impress."

"Thanks, Dad!" Grabbing the bill, he ran off to

join his new friends. She turned back to watch the band. Tommy laughed at something the other man said. She sighed. Even his laugh irritated her.

"Tommy, I'm ready to go home." Looking for Seth, her gaze traveled across the dance floor to the pavilion in the back.

She froze. There sat Jake. Their eyes met. He gave her a small salute before turning back to his companion. Had he been watching her?

Anjelica sat on the other side of the tall, round table. She looked beautiful in her peach sweater, a silk scarf tied high on her neck. Dark hair framed her pretty face.

She took a deep breath. Jake had every right to date whomever he wanted. He had a right to be happy. That's what he deserved.

She swallowed. If she had really changed, she couldn't be the mean girl anymore. No matter how much it hurt to see Jake with someone else.

Tommy leaned in and whispered, "Well, look who's here, your friend, Jake Torres. He appears to be on a date. Isn't she one of those Ortegas? There must be hundreds of them. Is she the one with all those scars and a boyfriend that died in Iraq?"

"Her name is Anjelica, and yes, she's Lupe and Santiago Ortega's daughter. It was her husband, and he was killed in Afghanistan. We sent flowers to the memorial."

He hugged her with his free arm and wrapped his hand around hers, pulling her in the direction of Jake and Anjelica. "This is one of the reasons we make such a good team. You remember all the details about people. Let's say hello."

Vickie wanted to drag her feet and decline, but not wanting to cause a scene, she followed. She snorted at her own thoughts. Last year all she did was cause scenes.

People wouldn't believe the change in her. God did work wonders when you let him. She smiled. Peace in the storm; she was getting there.

Tommy looked at her. "What?"

"Nothing. Lead on." Now if she could stick to her resolve to be a nicer person. It would have been easier from across the pavilion than sitting next to the girl dating Jake. She would always think of him as hers.

Vickie's muscles tightened, and she forced her mouth to stay in the shape of a smile; it might be a mask for now, but she'd get there. Determined to be nice, she followed Tommy. With God's help, she could do this.

Jake tried not to watch as Vickie and Tommy made their way toward the back of the pavilion. With each step, his worst fear came closer. He kept refocusing on Anjelica. Her sweet voice drifted in and out of his consciousness.

Tommy carried a sleeping Ashley as if it was the most natural thing for him to do. A burn started in the pit of Jake's stomach. This was the reason he had fled the day after graduation. He did not want to see Tommy in the life he wanted. Maybe Anjelica was ready to go home.

Tommy's little family stopped at his table. "Torres, how are you?"

Too late; he was trapped. Before Jake could answer, Vickie's ex turned his flashy smile to his date. "Anjelica, please accept my condolences and know your husband is a hero. The flowers we sent couldn't accurately express our sorrow for your loss."

Jake watched the joy in Anjelica's eyes disappear. She stopped tapping to the music and became still.

She answered with a simple "Thank you."

Ashley lifted her head and rubbed her eyes. "Officer Torres! Hello."

Jake couldn't help but smile back. Did Tommy have any idea the gifts he had been given? "Hello, Ashley. I like your pink boots. You're a great dancer, just like your mom. She used to dance like that."

"Vic's grown up now." Tommy narrowed his eyes, the smooth smile gone.

"Daddy, when I grow up, I'm still going to dance and wear pink boots everywhere. They match the toolbox Officer Torres gave me. I fixed my doll house." With one arm around her father's neck, she blinked a couple of times. "Daddy, I'm hungry and thirsty."

Tommy slipped her down until she stood on her own. "Can you wait?"

"Please, Daddy." She rubbed her eyes and yawned.

"In a minute, sweetheart. The adults are talking."

Vickie reached for her daughter. "I'll take her."

"No, I've got it. She just needs to learn to wait." He faced Jake again. "So Torres, all Seth has been talking about is this big father-and-son flag-football game next weekend."

Jake nodded. "You should be proud of him. He's really good on the line."

Tommy snorted. "There's no glory on the line. But I've got him covered. I donated to the building fund and volunteered to quarterback. Seth will be on my team. We'll show you and your boys some real football." He chuckled at his own joke; no one else laughed.

Vickie glared at her ex. "Tommy, we're just fellowshipping and raising some money for the youth building. No one is trying to prove anything. It's just for fun."

"Right. Torres, here, was one of the most competitive jocks I played against."

"We were on the same team, Miller."

"Excuse me, Daddy, can I please go now?" Ashley threaded her little fingers into her dad's larger ones.

Jake focused on a cut along the side of his thumb,

reminding himself he had no right to be jealous of the simple father and daughter touch.

Vickie reached for Ashley. "Let me take her."

"No, I've got her. Right, sweetheart?" He picked her back up and kissed her forehead. "We'll be right back."

Vickie stopped him before he left. "Can you get Seth so we can leave?"

"Sure, babe." He winked at her.

Jake sat back, making sure his muscles stayed relaxed, and suppressed a growl. He looked over the dance floor. The burn flared from his gut to his throat. He took a drink of his iced tea. How was he going to survive seeing them together?

"That color is beautiful on you." Vickie sat across from him, next to Anjelica at their small, round table.

Jake couldn't take his eyes off Vickie's hands as they peeled the corner of the label off her water bottle. She wasn't wearing her wedding ring.

Anjelica smiled at Vickie. "Thanks. I hear you're making all the dresses for Lorrie Ann's wedding. You have an incredible talent."

Vickie laughed. The sound tickled his ears. He glanced away, not wanting Anjelica to see a love-sick idiot looking at the wrong girl. He'd get over it; he had to.

"Anjelica," Vickie leaned in closer and rested her hand on the other woman's arm. "You're the talented one. Mother has two of your sculptures in the pool room."

He cleared his throat. He needed to concentrate on his date. "I didn't know you were an artist."

"Oh, not really. I do a few pieces here and there for fund-raisers." She turned back to Vickie. "You, Jake's mom and my mom are truly the talented ones. I don't even come close to your talents."

"You're right about your mom and Maria. The last fund-raiser I went to there was a bidding war over their baked goods."

"Oh, that's guaranteed, it gets crazy between her cakes and Maria's cookies. My sister's actually pushing them to start an online sweet-eats shop."

Shock startled Jake out of his self-debate over Vickie. "My mother, Maria? Online?" This is the first he had heard of this plan.

Anjelica's eyes widened. "I thought you knew. I'm sorry."

"No, it's a great idea. I just didn't know anything about it."

Vickie laughed. "Well, if she goes worldwide, she can't blackmail you with her cookies anymore. You could just buy them."

Anjelica's eyebrow went up. "Your mother blackmails you with cookies?"

Jake grinned and shook his head. "It's emotional torture, her last ditch effort to control me."

"Oh, that sounds like something my mother would do if she had that kind of leverage." She leaned in and smiled at him. "So is this what this date is really about? You getting a batch of chocolate chip cookies."

"Don't forget the pecans. That's his favorite part." Vickie crossed her arms over her chest and smiled at him.

He smiled back.

Anjelica looked around. "Umm…I need to find the little girls' room. I'll be right back."

Alone with Vickie, Jake couldn't think of anything polite to say. After a few minutes of silence, Vickie was the first to speak.

"She's a lot younger than us, isn't she? I barely remember her in school. Wasn't she in the sixth grade when we graduated?"

"Victoria, she's only a few years younger, but I would say her experiences make her more mature than either of us."

She took a deep breath and blew it out, causing her long bangs to dance. "You're right. I didn't mean any disrespect. Anyway, I owe you an apology." She closed her eyes for a long second. She looked right at him when she opened them back up. "What do I manage instead? I make a snide remark about your date." She chewed on her bottom lip, sucking it into her mouth as she looked toward the band. "I've never handled you with other girls very well. You've never even been mine, so I don't know why I do it. I'm sorry."

"I wanted to belong to you." *Wrong thing to say. Should have not said that.* "Sorry I…"

"Jake, how did we…"

They both paused, waiting for the other to talk.

Jake leaned forward, resting on his elbows and studied her profile. He couldn't do this, not here, not now. Maybe if he dealt with her and Tommy directly he could handle it better.

This twist in his gut needed to go. He'd treat her like an assignment. With facts and a plan. "So will you and Tommy stay in Clear Water or move back to Florida?"

That brought her attention back to him. "I'm staying here. I'm not sure what Tommy's doing. Jake, right now I have to think of Seth and Ashley. He's their father."

"I know you're doing the right thing." As much as it tore him up.

"Really? Because it doesn't feel like it." She reached for his arm. "Jake."

He jerked back. He couldn't take her touch right now; his resolve was too fragile.

She pulled her hands into her lap. The hurt in her eyes sliced at him. He wanted to undo his last action, but knew his heart couldn't afford it.

She rubbed her hand over her eyes, the one where her wedding ring should have been. "Jake, I owe you a huge apology. The other day in the barn." She looked down. "You're right. I had no right to be angry. You can't read my mind. I expected you to treat me like we were in a relationship." She raised her gaze to his. "The day Tommy showed up I was ready…"

"Stop." His heart physically slammed against his chest. "Don't say it. If you can't mean it now, then don't say it." He needed to get away from her.

To his relief he saw Anjelica make her way back to him. He stood and smiled. Her mouth pulled at the corners as she wrapped her arms around her middle.

"I love this song." Her voice, with a thread of longing, helped him focus on his date instead of his weakness.

"Then let's dance." He held out his arm and Anjelica wrapped her fingers around him.

"Sounds splendid." Joy sparkled in her dark eyes.

With a nod to Vickie, he led Anjelica through the crowd, away from his first love. He had to move on, the way other people managed it. Maybe he could find happiness with Anjelica.

As he turned her onto the dance floor, he saw Vickie sitting alone, watching him. She smiled and gave him a salute before disappearing. He missed a step.

"Oh, I'm sorry." Anjelica's voice penetrated the fog. "It's been so long since I've danced with anyone."

They bumped into a couple spinning around the floor. Jake mumbled an apology and guided his partner more to the center of the crowded dance area. Their feet collided again.

"I promise I know how to dance." He chuckled, looking down at their boots, trying to keep it light.

"No, it's me. I'm all stiff. When I was thirteen, Steve taught me to dance, and I only felt safe dancing with him." She lifted her chin to look up at him. "This is my first dance with anyone else."

"Are you sure you want to dance?"

She nodded her head. "Everyone tells me I need to get on with my life. It's been years."

"Anjelica, there's no time limit to grief."

She looked at him, moisture in her eyes and a smile on her lips. "Thank you. I'm glad you're my first date."

He turned and pulled her out of the way of the spinning couple. He saw Vickie with Tommy's arm around her and paused, causing another couple to bump into them.

"Sorry," he muttered to the passing couple.

"I'm ruining this song for you." He needed to focus on his date. His knee bumped into Anjelica's leg. He winced. "Sorry again."

Anjelica tilted her head, concern in her eyes. "I think I'm ready to head home. What about you?"

"Are you sure?" This was her first night out in years, and he was being a jerk, fawning over another woman.

"Yeah. I really enjoyed tonight. My mom's right.

I do need to get out more." She leaned in closer. "Don't tell her I said that."

He led her off the dance floor. "Your secret is safe with me. Maybe we could even try doing this again?"

She nodded and smiled. "As friends, yes, I think that would be nice." Anjelica glanced toward Vickie then back at him. "I have a feeling you don't stumble when you dance with her. I remember y'all in high school. You seemed so perfect together."

"We were just friends."

She laughed. "The kind of friends that made every girl jealous. We all thought you would have married. We were really surprised when you left for the marines and she married Tommy."

"Life has a way of changing your plans." Taking his gaze off Vickie, he glanced down at his partner for the night. "I guess you know that better than any of us."

"Yes, and life is too short to let fear stop us from living the fullest life God intended." Her head jerked down. "Sorry, I'm the last person that should be talking about someone else's life."

He patted her hand on his arm as he led her through the crowd, the lively music making it hard to hear.

"No, it's good."

His gaze scanned the area for Vickie and her

family. He couldn't find them. Grateful for the company and wise words, he steered Anjelica through the tables and headed for the exit gate.

# *Chapter Fifteen*

It had been a week since the disastrous date with Anjelica, and now he faced Tommy at the big annual father-and-son game. The brittle blades of parched grass cut into Jake's knuckles. The hard, dry ground gave no cushion. He absorbed the pain and focused all of it on Tommy. His goal…to take the enemy down.

One too many nasty remarks from father to son had pushed Jake over the edge. His eyes narrowed, watching Vickie's ex as he played quarterback. That's what he loved about football—he learned at an early age it was okay, even rewarded, when all the rage and anger were brought to the field. He could leave it all here.

Snap, charge. Vickie's ex scrambled back, fear flashing in his eyes. Jake pulled his flag, not breaking eye contact. Tommy glared at him.

Snap, charge. In Tommy's scramble this time he

tripped and fell on his backside. The ball useless on the ground.

Jake offered his hand, but it remained hanging, ignored.

Seth ran over. "Dad. Are you okay?"

Tommy brushed the grass and dust off. "Son, you've got to cut faster. I can't throw if you're not in the right place. We need a time-out."

Pastor John stood between the two men, blew the whistle and called a time-out. "You all right, Tommy?" He cut a look back to Jake with one eyebrow raised.

Jake shrugged his shoulder and went back to his team.

Adrian bumped him with his shoulder. "Do we need to make the hole bigger for you to get to him?"

Derrick, another teen in the mentoring program, looked over his shoulder. "What's up with that guy? Doesn't he know it's just a friendly game?"

Rhody's oldest son, Cash, shook his head. "No wonder Seth's always in a bad mood."

"I've had about enough of Tommy." Rhody shook his head. "When is he heading back to Florida?"

As much as Jake would love to pancake Tommy, it wouldn't help Seth. "Come on, guys. Let's focus on the game."

The whistle blew, and they lined up again. Jake adjusted his yellow flag and got back into position. He gave the sidelines a quick glance and found

Vickie still standing with her parents and Ashley. She had her arms crossed and a frown on her face.

Rhody yelled at his team. "Come on, boys, the brisket smells done to me. Let's get this game wrapped up."

Jake looked across the line and made eye contact with Seth. He smiled, hoping to encourage him. With each play Seth looked more nervous, less confident.

When the ball snapped this time, Jake held back a bit and waited for Seth to get in place before charging Tommy.

Enjoying the flash of fear in Tommy's eyes more than he should, Jake pulled up and grabbed a red flag. He turned in time to see Seth reach up and pull the ball down into his chest. But unfortunately, Derrick grabbed his red flag, stopping his forward movement.

"Good catch, Seth!" Vickie yelled from the side. Ashley jumped up and down. Seth tossed the ball to Pastor John, and smiling, he ran to his dad.

"Son, you've got to move faster. If you had twisted he couldn't have yanked your flag. Do you even want to win this game?"

Jake saw Seth's shoulders slump. He bit back a growl and took a step forward.

Adrian laid a hand on Jake's arm. "Want me to lay him flat this play?"

Relaxing his muscles, Jake smiled at his friend and shook his head. He checked his watch. Time was almost up. They'd get this over, and he'd have a one-on-one with Seth, and hopefully undo any harm Tommy had done.

People were still arriving for the dinner and bake sale. He noticed Anjelica walking from the parking lot, followed by his mother and her mother, Lupe. Each carried a large box that he knew would be filled with baked goods.

With a grunt Adrian's twin brother, George, snapped the ball. Distracted, Jake almost missed the play. Tommy stepped back and released the ball, sending it sailing high down the field. Seth cut to the left and lunged upward. It brushed the tips of his fingers, out of his reach. Flying past him, the ball landed right in Derrick's hands. Seth spun, immediately grabbing the yellow flag and stopping the play.

Proud of Seth for the quick action, Jake smiled... until he noticed Tommy rushing to the kid, an intense scowl pulling his face tight.

"It's not that hard to catch a ball." Tommy shoved Seth's smaller frame, knocking him to the ground. "Don't be a loser."

Rushing over, Jake placed himself between father and son. "Shove me. Push someone your own size." He stood with one foot forward, daring Tommy to come at him.

Seth pushed himself up out of the dirt. Men from both teams surrounded them.

He realized he didn't have to do this alone. Jake

took a deep breath and a step back, placing him next to Seth. "You all right, Seth?"

Head still down, the boy nodded. "I tripped."

Tommy's fist tightened at his side. "This is between me and my son. Get out of my way." With a harsh jerk to his arm he pointed to the ground next to him. "Seth, come here."

Jake put his left hand on Seth's shoulder. Before he could say anything else, Pastor John was between them again.

"I'm calling the game. The win goes to the Motley Crew."

"No, that was interference. I'm not losing just to serve everyone here."

George, who had been Tommy's center, placed a hand on his arm. "Come on, man. It was a good game. The losing team serves the dinner. It's tradition." He smiled and shrugged. "Let's go wash up. It'll be fun."

Tommy pulled away from George. "But we didn't lose. The game's not over. I'm not serving anyone."

Seth's father was embarrassing his whole family and didn't care. Jake's jaw started hurting. He glanced over to the sidelines.

Vickie looked like she was ready to charge the field. Her father had a hand on her arm.

He realized his own fists were so tight, the circulation seemed to stop. He turned back to Tommy. Pastor John's calmness saved Jake from anything rash.

"Tommy, maybe you need to leave. That's not how we treat kids or adults for that matter."

"No, I said I tripped. It was my fault." Seth's voice was small.

Jake put his hand on Seth's shoulder. "It's not your fault." He looked Tommy in the eye. "I think we all agree it's time for you to go."

Tommy looked at the faces around him before shouldering his way through the wall of men and boys.

Jake watched as the tall blond made his way to Vickie. Her face was full of justified rage.

He turned to Seth, still standing next to him. He needed to distract the kid while Vickie dealt with his dad. "Seth, you did a great job today. Don't let his insecurities make you feel like you did something wrong."

Adrian patted Seth on the back. "Good move, kid. There was no way you could have caught that last ball." Other men went out of their way to assure Seth he had done a great job.

The players started kidding each other as they moved to the food and drink area. Jake glanced over at Vickie. She looked up at Tommy, furious.

He smiled. Tommy deserved all her rage.

"Umm...Jake, can I ask you something?" Seth's voice was low.

Jake had to bend down to hear him. "Shoot."

Seth turned his head back and forth before speaking. "Is it stealing..." He ran his hand over his mouth. "I mean, what should you do if someone wants passwords? I can give mine right, but I shouldn't give Papa Jack's or Mom's."

"What kind of passwords are we talking about?"

Seth shrugged his thin shoulders. "Bank accounts and stuff like that, I guess. I don't know."

Jake cut his glance from Seth to Tommy, who now stood in front of a mad Vickie. He narrowed his eyes. It was a good thing they had finished the game. "Is your father asking for these passwords?"

The boy crossed his arms and tucked his head. "No! Forget it." Seth looked toward his parents. "They've been talking about passwords at school, and I was just wondering."

He placed his hands on the boy's narrow shoulder. "Seth, just because he's your dad doesn't mean he's above reproach. You do what's right and don't ever feel guilty for that."

Seth swallowed hard. His gaze stayed on his parents. "I think my mom's mad at him." He closed his eyes. "I've messed everything up."

"No. You played well. What he said and did to you was wrong, Seth. Just because he's your dad doesn't make him right. Your mom has every right to be angry." Jake tilted his head up. Gray clouds rolled across the sky. "It looks like we might get some rain. Come on, let's get a clean shirt and wash up. I believe you have some serving to do. I think both teams should serve today." Most of the area citizens were already sitting and eating the brisket and sausage plates. Some of the men walked around with pitchers of tea and water, serving the drinks.

The last thing Seth needed right now was to be in the middle of his parents' discussion.

Helping Seth get a pitcher, he walked with him through the tables, pouring iced tea. Jake noticed people made a point to tell Seth what a good job he had done on the field. He really loved this town.

Jake guided Seth to the large tables where his grandparents ate. He thought about the passwords and didn't like what his instincts were telling him.

For the last couple of weeks he had dismissed his suspicions of Tommy, afraid jealousy had clouded his judgment. Seth's father had always been selfish but had he crossed the line to criminal? After hearing Seth's questions, he had a few calls to Florida he needed to make tonight. Something was fishy, and he wanted facts before he spoke with Vickie.

"This was supposed to be a fun father-and-son game."

Her mother wrapped her arm around Vickie's waist and leaned in to whisper, "I've never seen him be so mean."

"Mother, you only saw Tommy with the kids a few times and most of that was for his campaign."

"Oh, Vickie, I'm so sorry. I thought you were just embellishing. What do we do?" She moved to Vickie's other side, huddled between her and her husband. "J.W., you need to do something." Elizabeth stepped back. "I'm going to help with the bake sale."

"Mother?"

Her mother cut a look to Ashley. "To remain a good Christian woman, I need to remove myself from the situation." She held her hand out to Ashley. "Sweetheart, come help Grandma set up the baked goods. I'll get you a cookie."

"Can I, Mommy?" Unaware of the drama, Ashley danced around her grandmother.

Vickie nodded, relieved that her mother was taking her daughter out of hearing range, but she was also irritated with her. After years of advocating for Tommy, she was going to hide now?

Her father leaned in and whispered, "Sweetheart, I'm going with your mother because I might hit him, and that won't do you any good. You're not alone. We are all close by."

"Thank you, Daddy."

Tommy approached them, holding out his hand to her father. "J.W., how's it going?"

"Don't mess with my family," her father said before turning and leaving Tommy's hand hanging in the air.

He glared at Vickie. "What did you tell him?"

Despite the chill in the air, uncomfortable warmth crawled over Vickie's skin. "Nothing. Your actions spoke for themselves."

His eyes went wide in real confusion. "My actions? Your son embarrassed me. He can't even catch a ball. Did you see how many opportunities I gave him?"

"He just wanted to play football with friends. You turned it into something about you." She took a deep breath and sent a prayer for calmness. "This is not what the kids need."

He sighed and tugged at the neck of his T-shirt. "You're right. This is not a good environment for the kids." He reached for her hand, gripping it in his. "Vickie, let's get this over with and head back to Florida. We can show your father we mean to make this work. But I can't do it here. Too many petty jealousies, and Torres is always trying to make me look bad."

"I think you do that all on your own." She yanked hard to free her hand. "Over two years ago you signed the papers, telling me that we weighed you down. Now you're weighing us down. It's over, Tommy. I would rather you not visit the kids anymore."

"No. You can't do that." He wrapped his fingers around her upper arm. "Everything we ever wanted is right in our grasp. We just need your father's support." He glared at Jake. "This is his fault."

The fury in his eyes scared her. Out of the corner of her vision, she saw Jake frown and take a step toward them. "Tommy, please, people are watching." Tommy had never let his composure slip in public before, and it frightened her. The last thing her children needed was a public drama. If Tommy did anything, she knew her father and Jake would be all over him.

She didn't want her children to feel they had to pick sides.

To her relief, he dropped his arm, relaxed and smiled a smile he spent hours practicing in front of the mirror. A measured calmness in his voice. "Vickie, why do you have to push me? All our dreams are about to come true."

"What dreams are those, Tommy?" she asked. "I'm confused. All I ever wanted was a family to take care of, in a home we filled with love."

"You can have that. Business is great. I just need a little more capital to push it over the top. Then the world will be ours. I'll get you out of this hick town and into a house bigger than our last one. You and the kids deserve the best schools, cars and clothes. We can travel." He stepped closer, slower this time and rubbed his hand up her arm. "I know you want more kids. You can do whatever you want."

"You have no clue about my dreams. I love this town. All I ever wanted was a family and to be part of a community. I want to raise our children here."

He narrowed his eyes. "It's Torres, isn't it? He's been telling you lies about me."

"He hasn't said anything about you. He's giving me space to make the right decision. You wanted the divorce, and I decided to let it stand. You need to apologize to Seth then leave."

"What? He owes me an apology." He looked to

the tent where everyone gathered to eat. "You're babying him."

Vickie knew what she needed to do and her stomach twisted in a knot. "Tommy, you need to leave. Don't come to the house without an invitation. Don't contact the kids unless you talk to me first."

"This is ridiculous, Vic. We're on the verge of getting back together. I'm a new man."

"That's why you shoved Seth to the ground, because you turned over a new leaf? I don't like this new leaf, Tommy."

"Give me another chance." He leaned in closer, both hands wrapped around her arms.

She stepped back. "You called me and said you're getting married. Your son was so upset that he ran away. He was airlifted to the hospital, and you were too busy to bother with us. Then you suddenly show up at my door expecting us to be one big, happy family again? You haven't changed. You still use and manipulate people to get what you want. What is it this time? Money from Daddy? You just said you needed a little more capital. Has all the loving father, husband routine been about you needing more money?" All the pieces fell into place now, the big gestures, the gifts. "You need money."

"Your father owes me." His jaw shut tight.

"How? When I got pregnant with Seth, he paid

for you to finish law school. He never asked for a penny to be paid back."

"Yeah, well, when I ran for Senate he could have gotten me more support with his contacts, but he didn't. I ended up losing and bankrupt."

"You made poor decisions and *we* ended up bankrupt." She sighed, realizing the irony of the last fight she had with Jake mirrored this one with Tommy. Jake was right. She was still dragging her anger about Tommy around with her, letting it shadow her relationship with Jake. "This is getting nowhere. If you refuse to apologize to Seth, then leave." She crossed her arms over her chest. The knots disappeared, and her shoulders were lighter. She made the right choice. Tommy was poison.

He glanced over to the gathering then back to her. Putting his face closer to her, he sneered. "This is not over."

The sky got darker as gray clouds blocked the sun. Vickie looked up. Maybe it would finally rain. She could use the cool relief of a heavy storm. Tommy stalked to his car.

# Chapter Sixteen

The food had no taste. Jake kept his attention on the people around him, afraid to watch the couple he tried to ignore.

An interesting group had gathered at this table to say the least. Vickie's parents sat on his left side of the table and his mother on his other arm. Anjelica and her mother sat across from them with Seth and Ashley next to her.

Seth shoved the last of his tortilla in his mouth. "Papa Jack, can I eat my dessert at Pastor John's table? I'd like to thank him for letting me play."

J.W. grinned at the boy. "And there happens to be an empty seat next to his daughter. That's convenient."

Seth turned red. The second his grandfather nodded his approval, he jumped up and was gone.

Elizabeth laid her napkin over her plate. "Maybe that will help him forget his father's behavior today." Her glance slid over to where Vickie and Tommy still stood.

Jake's gaze followed. Vickie crossed her arms. A grim look hardened her face. Tommy grabbed her by the upper arm, pulling her toward him. Jake stood. Anger fired his blood.

Vickie's mother laid a hand on his arm. "She's got this. If you go now it will just cause more problems. He won't…" She turned her head to Ashley and smiled. "Here, sweetheart, take this money over to the donation basket." Once the little girl skipped away, Elizabeth leaned close to Jake and whispered, "Vickie will do the right thing and make sure he is no longer part of this family."

Years of resentment threatened to bubble up from his gut. However, he agreed Vickie could handle her ex for now. "I thought you were on team Tommy."

"After today? I think not." Her perfectly maintained and painted face tight, her chin up, she said, "His behavior with Seth was inexcusable."

So it's okay for him to push her daughter around but she draws the line at her grandson. He kept his thoughts to himself, biting back the bitter words he wanted to spew.

He would not take his eyes off Vickie now. If Tommy dared to touch her, it would be for the last time. He glanced at J.W. Vickie's dad sat on the edge of his seat.

"Don't worry, Jake. He won't mess with her here.

But I think it's time she took some legal action. Maybe move back to our house."

Jake tracked Tommy as he stalked to his car and drove off. Then he allowed his chest to loosen. His breath came a little easier.

Elizabeth reached for her husband's arm. "He would never really hurt her or the kids." She glanced at Jake. "Would he?"

Jake didn't answer her. He kept his gaze on Vickie as she made her way to their table. A tight smile plastered on her face as the wind pushed her loose hair around. *God, You know how much I love her. What do You want me to do about it?*

Jake bit down; his jaw muscles flexed until they hurt. He had his suspicion that Tommy was on the edge of being desperate. From his experience, a desperate man made a very dangerous man.

A part of Vickie felt freed, but another waited. Tommy had made a promise he would be back. For the first time she was scared of him. As she got closer to the tables, Anjelica waved her over.

"Vickie, come sit with us. I saved some desserts for Jake, but there's plenty for you, too."

This day just got better and better. First she allowed Tommy to humiliate their son and now she would have to watch Anjelica and Jake flirt. She sat on the chair across from Jake and grabbed a butterfly cupcake. She ate the wings first.

Jake laughed at something Anjelica said to his

mother. Her eyes darted to the scarf tied around her neck. Even she wasn't low enough to hold the scars against her. Knowing Jake's love for the underdog, he probably found them attractive.

Vickie bit the little heart-shaped head off and chewed. Anjelica would make a better wife and mother, anyway.

Vickie excelled at messing up and saying the wrong thing. She had no business even contemplating a relationship with Jake. Jake needed someone gentle and loving.

Anjelica always had a kind word for everybody. She would never utter bitter, hateful words at the pastor's fiancée. If Anjelica had a son, he would never steal from the local grocery store or run away with the pastor's daughter.

Anjelica's mother and Jake's mother beamed at their children. Lupe loved Jake and was Maria's best friend. Yeah, Jake and Anjelica made a perfect match, and someday they would have perfect children. She wanted to cry.

The women started gathering the empty plates, and Maria turned to her son. "I'm going to Lupe's house to work on our website."

He chuckled and looked at Anjelica. "My mother, the online entrepreneur." He reached for a cookie. "Can I take the leftovers home?"

"I'll take them to your truck on the way out," Anjelica offered, so politely.

Vickie closed her eyes and told herself to behave.

Tommy had put her in a bad mood, and she was close to falling into the old pattern of taking it out on others. Her words could either hurt or heal. She prayed for God to remove the anger.

Jake's mother slapped his hand. "Oh, no, you don't." She picked up her handbag and crossed her arms. "You know the rules. But if you want to buy them there's nothing I can say about that. Anjelica is taking the money."

The perfect woman gave a perfect laugh. "Poor Jake. You have to buy your own mother's cookies. That is so unfair."

Vickie gritted her teeth at the sweet sound. She grabbed a second cookie, a ladybug, and bit the head off. Ugh, there had to be *something* wrong with the woman.

Anjelica didn't know Jake the way she did. "Yeah, his mother is blackmailing him with cookies because he won't give her grandchildren. You seem the best candidate."

Maria gasped. Jake glared at her. *Drat.* She bit her lip. There she went again, saying things she shouldn't.

Laughter erupted from Anjelica. "You're so funny, Vickie."

Everyone smiled again, everyone but Vickie and Maria.

Lupe slapped Jake's shoulder. "We mothers will do whatever it takes to see our children settled and happy."

Anjelica patted Vickie's hand. "From what I've seen, it might not be too long."

Well, that was it. Jake was moving faster than she thought. Is this what he felt when he heard she was marrying Tommy? Had his gut twisted at the thought of her being with someone else? She couldn't breathe. The thought of losing Jake at this point just about undid her resolve not to cry. Even though she knew it was what she deserved. She had to trust God. He was in control, not her.

She stood, knocking her chair over.

Anjelica reached over to pick up the metal chair. "Are you okay?"

Making sure to smile, Vickie nodded. She moved away from everyone and started to roll up the tablecloths.

Jake followed and watched her in silence for a moment. She ignored him. He reached across and stopped her fingers from working with his dark hand. "Vickie, are you all right?"

She would be if everyone would stop asking her that. "Yes. It's just been a long day, and I need to gather the tablecloths and centerpieces."

"Can I help?" Anjelica stood next to Jake.

Jake's little girlfriend asked so kindly. Vickie sighed. At least she kept her snarky comments to herself. That was an improvement. *Right, God?*

"No, I got it. I think they're waiting for you."

"Oh, I didn't get a chance to talk to you about

your sewing project. I would love to join y'all. Can I come to the next meeting?"

Vickie managed the most pleasant look she could fake. "That would be great."

"Good. I'll see you then." With a big smile, Anjelica picked up the box of cookies and turned to Jake. "I'll put these in your truck. You don't have to pay."

"Oh, no, my mother will find out somehow."

When Jake opened his wallet to pull the money out a blue piece of paper fell to the table, unnoticed. He handed the bills over to Anjelica.

Vickie picked it up to give it back to him. Looking down, she noticed the name. Fisting the paper, she waited for the pretty brown-haired woman to leave.

"See you later."

"Bye." Anjelica waved to them then ran after her mother.

"You dropped this. It's Anjelica's number." She smiled at him, hoping to hide the disappointment. "She's a very pretty girl." She kept her eyes focused on the paper as his hand slipped it from her fingers.

"Yeah, she is that." He chuckled. "And very sweet."

"That's true. You deserve sweet." He did. He did, he really did.

"I prefer a little spice myself." He winked at her before turning away to the other end of the table.

Was she spice? Had she read the whole situation wrong? "You seemed to be getting along at the music festival." Why did she torture herself?

His shoulders shrugged under his T-shirt. "We did. Her mother is worse than mine when it comes to pushing her to date. She hasn't even been out with friends in the last few years."

"Oh." Not sure what to say, she chewed her lips. "So you're friends, like us."

He laughed and flipped the table onto its side. "No." With his hands braced on the edge, he leaned forward. "Another friend like you just might kill me." Lifting the table, he hit the metal legs to fold them under. "That was the first time she's gone out since Steve's death. You should call her. I think a girls' night out would be good for her."

Was he serious? She found herself smiling a little. Knowing Jake, he was. He always saw the best in people, even her, especially her. She couldn't imagine losing everything Anjelica had at such a young age and still believing in God's goodness.

Okay, so she would get over her petty jealousy and look at everyone through love's eyes. She could be a better person, even without Jake.

Vickie ran her finger along the edge of the table. "Did you know she was about seven months pregnant when she got the news of his death?"

He paused. "So she didn't just lose her husband," he murmured.

Placing the tablecloths and centerpieces in the box, she looked up at Jake. "A couple of months later the baby was stillborn. I don't know why she never talks about it. I don't understand why life has to be so unfair." With a hard jerk, she flipped the table on its side and folded the legs.

Jake still stood with the table in his grasp. He shook his head. "We can't understand God's plan, but we can have faith that He loves us. I wish I had some words of wisdom, but I'm about as dry as the ground around here." He took the tables from her and lined them against the pole where the other volunteers had started stacking them. "Last week in church, John talked about rejoicing in our suffering. Sometimes you have to wonder how much character building we really want."

Great! If the goal was to build character, then she still had a great deal of suffering to look forward to, and she had better learn to rejoice instead of blame. She wished she had Jake's faith. "You seem so steady all the time."

He winked at her and began tossing tables into the bed of his truck. They continued to work in silence.

Pastor John pulled his blue, work-worn Ford next to the tent. With the window down, he rested his arm on the door. "Thanks for helping out. Rhody and his boys have all the chairs. I've got a truck-load of tables. George and the youth group will be coming back to take down the canopies. Do you mind getting these last tables to the church?"

"No problem." Jake walked over to the truck.

"The centerpieces looked great as always, Vickie." He slipped a green Jolly Rancher in his mouth. Concern creased his brow. "Are you all right?"

If one more person asked her that question, she'd scream. Instead, she nodded and gave him a tight smile. If nothing else, her mother taught her how to make things look nice.

He slapped his palm against the door a couple of times. "If you need anything, even just someone to talk to, call me anytime. Okay?"

"Thanks." She quickly turned and gathered more of the decorations. She didn't look back as Pastor John pulled off. Her mother would be shocked by her rudeness, but right now, she barely kept it together. Tommy, her parents, Seth, Jake, everywhere she turned there was more proof of her bad choices. Her chest hurt. If the pastor had said one more nice thing to her, it would have all broken loose. She could not afford to let that happen because she might not be able to get it back together.

Jake knew Vickie was on the edge but didn't know what to say without pushing her over.

She shrieked. He saw her finger pinched between the table and truck. Pulling her hand free, she wrapped it in her other, holding it tightly against her stomach. White teeth bit down on her bottom lip to the point Jake was worried she'd break the skin.

Dropping the table, he reached for her. She twisted away and shook her hand. "Stupid table." With her left foot she kicked the hard plastic top.

"Here, let me see." He reached for her hand again.

"No, I'm fine." She barely got the words out. Her eyelids fluttered.

"Stop being stubborn and give me your hand."

"I don't need your help, or anybody else's. I'm fine." With the last word, a sob escaped.

Not allowing her to argue, Jake pulled her into his arms. "It's okay. No one's here. It's just you and me."

"I've been so stupid." She dug deeper into his chest. She covered her face with her hands. "I let him back into our lives, and he hurt Seth." Her sobs cut off any more words as giant gulps came from her lungs.

Jake wished he had a way to protect her and the kids. He was going to have to trust God on this one.

"Hush." His arms engulfed her, pressing her against his heart, a heart that was breaking into pieces. His Vickie never cried. He stroked her hair, the silk strands inviting him to hide in their thickness. He continued to whisper in her ear.

His cheek touched the top of her head. The minutes slipped by. Maybe they could stay here forever and not have to deal with any of their problems.

The heavy weeping descended into sniffles. With a deep sigh, Vickie stepped away from him.

"I'm so sorry, that was—" she sniffed "—uncalled for." She wiped at the wet spots on his shirt.

He watched her hands dab his chest. Capturing her pale fingers in his dark hand, he stilled her movements. "Don't ever apologize for real emotions. We are way past that hang-up."

"I promised no more drama in my life. Today was not the day I wanted for my kids." She pulled free and rubbed her hands over her face.

"That was Tommy's drama. Not yours or the kids'. You are strong." He cupped her jaw in his large hands. "Thank you for not coming out on the field, by the way. I know it was difficult to stay on the sidelines, but Seth did well handling himself, and I think he got the support he needed from the other guys."

She massaged her fingers and snorted. "For a flag game it got a little physical."

His heart lightened a bit at her smile.

A small glimmer returned to her eyes. "Hopefully, Tommy will leave now," she said.

Jake had a feeling Tommy wasn't leaving without something from Vickie, but until he made the call to his friend and fellow former marine, Brad, he needed to wait before saying anything. Brad worked as a P.I. in Florida.

"Vickie, promise me you'll call if anything seems off. Don't worry about bothering me or that you're overreacting. Just call."

"After our talk, I really think Tommy's heading back to Miami."

He prayed that was true but had a bad feeling. Tommy had lied about a bunch of things. "Just promise me. Okay?"

With a sigh, she patted his arm. "Yes, sir. I promise to call."

"Come on, we don't want to get caught unloading in the rain." Jake tossed the last table into his truck bed.

Vickie sighed and put the box of decorations in the backseat. The cheerful colored material mocked the disaster her life had become. The harder she worked at standing on her own the more life seemed to push her down.

She paused. Her hand on the door handle. Maybe that was the problem. She was trying to control everything and everyone.

Closing her eyes, she prayed. Prayed to let it go and turn it all over to God.

"Vickie?" Jake stood next to her. "You sure you're okay?"

She shook her head and gave him a smile. "I will be."

Thunder rolled across the hills as the clouds assembled and twisted in the sky.

# Chapter Seventeen

At the Wednesday night prayer meeting, Jake followed his mother into the fellowship hall carrying the cookies he'd been forbidden to eat. While he sat in the truck waiting for his mother, Brad had called.

Now an ugly anxiety had him searching for Vickie. He needed to talk to her. He thought about calling her, but this information needed a personal, face-to-face delivery. He handed the tray to Maggie behind the counter, scanning the room for Vickie.

The conversation with Brad convinced him that Tommy could be dangerous. Life in Miami was not as good as old Tommy boy had made it out to be.

Instead of Vickie, he found the man he wanted to avoid. He rolled his head back to stretch his neck then popped his knuckles. The ex-husband walked up to him. With a wink at Maggie, Tommy stole one of his mother's cookies.

"What are you doing here, Tommy? I didn't think small-town prayer meetings were your thing."

He shrugged. "When it serves a purpose."

Jake leaned in and lowered his voice. "I've been talking to some law-enforcement friends of mine in Florida. You have a few projects you need to clean up down there."

Tommy's eyes narrowed. "I've been doing some of my own investigating, Mr. Choirboy. Seems you're not as perfect as you want everyone to believe." He stepped closer. "You're not getting my wife."

Frustrated, Jake took a measured step back. "She's not your wife, and I don't have time for your games. Do you have something to say?"

"Oh, I've plenty to say, but I'll wait to tell the right people."

"You have a good evening, then. I have things to do."

"Go right ahead. I've got things to do, too. Number one is getting my wife back." Tommy took a bite of the cookie and saluted Jake with a flip of his hand. "Your play for her is over. Before this little Bible study is done, she and this whole town are going to know the truth."

Jake clenched his fists. Done with this conversation, he turned to find Vickie.

Tommy had a new desperation about him that Jake didn't like. The fellowship hall started filling up with people coming in from the church. He spotted Vickie and her kids by the back door.

On his way to them, people kept stopping him,

congratulating Jake on the decision to run for sheriff. He didn't know who leaked the information, but he kept explaining that a decision had not been made yet.

Along with the discussion of the drought and hope for rain, it took Jake longer to get across the room than he wanted. When he finally stepped up behind her, she was talking with Anjelica and Yolanda.

Yolanda saw him first. "Hi, Jake."

Vickie turned and moved to the other side of Yolanda, leaving him next to Anjelica.

"Hello, ladies. Vickie, can we step outside to talk?"

"Me? I thought you were making your way to Anjelica." Running a hand up to the base of her throat, her gaze darted around the room. "Is it Seth? What has he done?"

Obviously, she had been watching him while pretending not to. Jake grinned at her. "Seth's fine. As far as I know, anyway."

A confused look crossed Anjelica's face. "Why would he be looking for me?"

"Well, aren't you dating?" Vickie asked.

"What?" A sharp yelp came from Yolanda.

Anjelica looked at Jake, her brows in deep creases. "She thinks we're dating?"

Jake shoved his hands in his front pockets and rolled his head back before looking at her. "I really never know what she's thinking."

Anjelica placed her hand on Yolanda's arm. "Well, I think I'm going to see if they need more coffee brewed. Yolanda, you want to help?" She jerked her head in the direction of the kitchen.

Yolanda looked confused as she glanced at Jake then back to Vickie. "Why would you think he was dating her?"

Anjelica grabbed her hand. "Bye."

"But we just made... Oh, right, coffee and tea. We need more tea. Well, see you later, Vickie, Jake."

They stood in silence. Vickie leaned forward and whispered, "So the lack of communication is always my fault? Mr. Marine turned sheriff."

At least she waited for the others to leave before saying anything. He smiled. She was changing. "You're right. I don't always tell you things that are going on with me. I wanted to give you room to make your own choices."

For a moment, she looked startled. He tried to recall if he had ever admitted being wrong to Vickie before. He didn't have the problem in other areas of his life. Maybe he changed a bit, too. Her silence didn't last long, though. Hand on her chest, she continued in her hushed voice. "Give me room? You left without a word. That's choosing for me. You didn't give me a choice, you ran." Her voice still low, she stared him in the eye.

He didn't see anger or bitterness but real confusion. He ran his fingers through his hair, knocking off his sunglasses. With a heavy sigh, he picked them up and hooked them on his front pocket. He wanted her to understand. The problem? He wasn't sure he understood his own actions. "I didn't want to force you. I thought it would be better if I didn't confront you."

"Not one time in our past did I feel forced. If anything, you backed off so quickly I thought I was doing the chasing. I thought you didn't want me. It's the same now, Jake. I can't read you."

He licked his dry lips, trying to find the right words. Not want her? All he ever wanted was her. "Victoria, I thought, no, I feared, losing control if you told me you wanted Tommy. I didn't want to be…" He didn't want to be what? Like his father? He was afraid of being his father. *God, I let fear stop me from seeing Your gifts.*

The epiphany stunned him. His mother was right. God had been trying to tell him, but his pride and guilt had not allowed God to deliver His promise.

"You didn't want to be what, Jake? Please talk to me."

"I will. I promise. We'll sort this out." He would give up running for sheriff if that's what she wanted. "First we need to get everything with Tommy settled." He glanced around the crowded room. "I have some information we need to discuss now."

She stood straighter and blinked. His chest tightened. Wow, she was beautiful. His throat went dry, and a nervous cough forced its way up.

He knew they were on the verge of something life altering. They might not be able to go back to the days of their childhood, but if they found a way to leave the past behind and trust God, they could have something even better. He needed to trust God in all things.

*God, thank You for bringing this amazing woman into my life. Please make me worthy.*

Vickie rested her fisted hands on her hips and glared at him. "Why are you looking at me so strangely?"

He cleared his thoughts. "I called a former marine friend in Florida."

Before he could finish, Tommy clapped to get everyone's attention. He stood on the low platform in front of the fellowship hall. Jake narrowed his gaze. There was no way Tommy would cause a scene at a church meeting. Even he wasn't that low. Next to him Vickie gasped, and tension rolled off her.

"What is he doing here?"

He stood closer, ready to protect her if need be.

"Good evening, neighbors and friends. Pardon the interruption to the social, but I just found some shocking information on one of our trusted citizens. A man you might want to support for sheriff."

At this point, the silenced crowd started murmuring. Some cast glances his way, others looked to the man standing behind Tommy, the man that had him wanting to run for the office to begin with, Ryan Vanderbilt.

"Jake?" A soft hand gripped his.

Jake's gut twisted. He scanned the room for his mother's small form. There was no way Tommy could have uncovered their secret. He took a deep breath, slowing the rush of his blood back down to a normal rate.

Pulling his hand out of Vickie's, he started across the room toward his mother. Lupe, Anjelica, Maggie and Yolanda stood around her. Would they stay there if the truth his mother had worked so hard to hide came out?

"I don't know about you but I would not trust a man with a violent background to protect this wonderful community." He paused as everyone got quiet again. "Before they moved to Clear Water, Jake Torres gave a loaded gun to his mother. She used that weapon to murder her husband, and Jake stood by as it happened."

With a unified gasp, the crowd turned to the small woman who had been serving their community for twenty years. Jake shot a look to his mother, her dark brown skin had lost color. Her shame exposed.

Jake's worst nightmare came to life. The blood rushed so hard he couldn't hear anything. He couldn't move. Censure covered the faces of the people around him. He needed to make sure his mother was okay. His proud mother stood straight, but he could tell tears threatened her stoic face. Much to his relief, Maggie and Lupe immediately wrapped their arms around her. Their fierce glares reminded him of warriors as they stared down Tommy.

Pastor John had cut across the room and stopped next to Vickie's ex. "Tommy, this is God's house and we will not allow slander here. It's time for you to leave."

Tommy sneered at the pastor. "I thought you preached 'the truth will set you free.'" He swung his arm over the crowd. "How will these God-fearing people know the truth if you shut me up?"

John took a step forward. "Leave, now."

Jake had worked so hard to become a man of honor in order to prove he was good enough. He saw Seth, now standing next to Vickie. If he truly wanted to be a man of integrity, as he told Seth, it was time he stepped up and told the whole truth.

"Pastor John." People parted as Jake walked to the platform. "I agree we do need the truth."

He turned so he could force himself to make eye contact with each person in the room. After a moment of heavy silence, he took a deep breath and started talking about a secret buried since he was nine years old.

"Living with my alcoholic father, Mother had gotten good at defusing violent situations. She learned to hide things in order to survive—money, alcohol, guns. One night when I was a child my father came in angry with a neighbor, accusing the man of flirting with my mother. Screaming, he demanded she hand over his guns."

His throat had gone dry. His heart rate accelerated as he remembered the feeling of being helpless. He had to get it all out.

"She refused to tell him where they were hidden. He didn't stop shouting, and his words turned to grabbing, kicking and hitting." The images and sounds flooded his brain. He continued at a slower pace, each word standing alone. "She knew he would kill the other man, so she took it without saying a word."

He made a show of looking in the eyes of everyone there, but too deep in the past to actually see them.

"Esmi, my little sister, was four at the time. When she woke up crying, he became angrier." Jake took a deep breath and sought out his mother. Trails of silent tears ran down her face.

They had spent so many years not talking about that night, but it had always hovered around them, never far. "I didn't know how to stop him. She had been in the hospital with a broken arm and ribs before, but this time it seemed worse, until he left the room."

He closed his eyes for a moment. The helplessness of that little boy became his again. For a brief second, he was small and useless.

"I remember praying he'd never come back." He

scanned the faces for a second time and now saw horror. His back teeth bit down hard until it hurt. He would lose all the respect he had worked so hard for all these years. He knew he had to tell the whole truth; no longer would he allow his mother to take the blame for him.

"I heard him in the kitchen, digging through drawers. Mother pulled herself up from the floor. She told me to take Esmi to the neighbors. Instead, I ran to get a gun." He swallowed. "Grabbing ammo and loading it, I went back to the kitchen. I just wanted to scare him, to make him leave my mother alone. He yelled at the baby to shut up then he lunged at my mother, a large butcher's knife in his hand." He took a deep breath. "I shot him. I pulled the trigger three times."

He sucked air deep into his lungs. If confession was good for the soul, he should feel a great deal better than he did. His gaze darted around the fellowship hall, finding condemnation in the stunned silence.

Mrs. Miller, the Dragon Lady herself, slammed her cane to the floor, demanding his attention. Her scowl made her face more disapproving than normal. "Officer Torres, why did Tommy say your mother killed the...her husband?"

"When I opened my eyes and saw all the blood and my father gasping for breath, I ran to the bathroom becoming brutally sick. My mother called 911 and told them she had shot him. She was afraid there might be charges and didn't want me to be in trouble." He made eye contact with the brave woman he loved more than his own life. She stood straight, sadness in each tear that ran down her timeless face. She deserved to be free of his burden.

"When they arrived, she told them the same thing. With her bruises and broken ribs along with the knife he still had, they reported it as self-defense and didn't question her more. I was only nine. I don't remember much after that. By the end of the week, she moved us here. She wanted to start over without his abuse or death shadowing our future."

He smiled at his mother. Speaking the words had freed the thoughts and emotions trapped in the dark corners of his mind. "She brought us here so my father's rage would not be our story. I'm very proud of her strength." He coughed, his throat raw. His gaze skipped all the familiar faces to find his mother once again.

She bit her lip and nodded to him with the smile that told him everything would be fine.

"I was a child, but I think I'm old enough now to stop hiding. If this makes me unfit to be your sheriff, I understand."

The silence faded as people started talking. The Dragon Lady stomped her cane to the hard floor. "Don't be ridiculous. A sheriff should protect those weaker and not go around talking about other people's business. You would be the perfect sheriff, young man. You just need a wife."

Laughter broke the quiet tension. For a moment, Jake wasn't sure if he heard right. People surrounded him, encouraging him. He heard comments about his bravery.

In a frantic movement, he looked for his mother. She smiled at him, her friends surrounding her.

He had confessed his greatest sin, and his world had not collapsed. His friends still respected him.

Turning from his mother, he sought Vickie. Her opinion mattered more than the whole town's. Would he lose her all over again before he had even won her? Would she see this as one more lie?

There she was. His heart rate picked up. Arms over her chest, she still stood where he left her. He saw what he dreaded most, disgust. He had lost her. So they weren't going to have that talk about their future.

Gritting his teeth, he nodded to the people around him, not hearing a word. He wanted to get his mother and leave. That thought caused him to pause.

Vickie had accused him of running whenever he doubted her. Instead of heading to the door, he turned to the only woman he had ever loved. She now stood with her arms around her daughter, talking with her parents.

He would make himself talk with Vickie, no more evading. If she didn't want him in her life anymore, she would have to tell him herself. He wasn't going to hide.

He sighed and ran his fingers through his hair. Tommy remained a threat. Glancing around the room, he realized his nemesis was nowhere to be seen. Where had he disappeared to? A new knot formed in the pit of Jake's stomach. Seth was gone, too.

# *Chapter Eighteen*

After all the times he had preached honor and truth, Seth probably took this hard. No telling how that fragile boy perceived the revelations tonight.

With one last glance at Vickie, Jake went outside to find Seth.

Standing alone at the end of the drive, Seth looked lost. Thick clouds blocked the crescent moon. He couldn't make out the boy's face.

"Seth?"

"Leave me alone."

Jake stayed a step back, not wanting to embarrass him. He was sure the boy had been crying. "I'm not leaving. I'm going to stay right here until you're ready to go back inside." Jake bit his lip. "I'm here, too, if you want to talk or have any questions."

In the distance, thunder rumbled. Humidity hung heavy in the air.

Seth rubbed his arm across his face. "You lied." His voice low and tense.

Jake didn't want to guess which lie Seth accused him of telling. "Which part upset you the most?"

"You told me a real man always tells the truth, even when it's hard."

"Yes. It's easier to talk about the right thing than actually doing it." Being totally open with Vickie's son was harder than talking to the whole town. "Seth, I messed up. All I can do now is admit it and claim the responsibility for my actions. That secret I carried ate away at me." He slipped his fingers in the back pockets of his jeans. Surrounded by darkness and empty streets, Jake struggled to organize any thoughts that would help Seth follow the right road. *God, this young man's heart is hurting. Please give me the words to help him heal.*

"Seth, fear of what other people thought kept me from completely living the life God had for me. I allowed my mother to cover up my action."

Seth twisted, looking up at Jake. The willowy moonlight slid through the clouds, highlighting his young face. "You murdered your father. How do you live with that?"

A punch straight to the gut. "Good question." How did he live with the knowledge he had shot his own father? "I was young, scared. He was trying to kill my mother. We always have some sort of excuse, but at the end of the day we have to step up and claim our actions." He took a heavy breath. "For twenty years I buried that memory, what I let my mom do for me. I have to honestly say for the first time I feel free of the burden."

"If you could go back would you do it differently?" The sincerity he found in the young boy's eyes forced him to really think about the answer and not just give a glib response.

"Wow, that's another good question." He took a deep breath and swallowed. For so many years he had refused to think about that night, his father's angry words, his little sister crying in fear, the sound of his mother's body being broken.

A light mist started falling from the sky, creating trails down his face. He wiped it dry. "Maybe I could have held the gun on him while my mother called the police, but no one had come to help in the past so I felt we were alone. I didn't have the training I have now. I did what I thought I had to do at the time to stop him from hurting my mother and sister." He looked back to the fellowship hall. The warmth of the light and faint sounds of people reassured him he was not completely alone anymore.

In a window, he saw his mother surrounded by her friends. "Truthfully, my biggest guilt came from my not caring that my father was gone. He was my father. I should have felt something other than relief." The irony of this conversation didn't slip past him. It should have happened years ago with this boy's mother. "Now I regret not being open about my past. Does that help you?"

"It doesn't matter. You all lie, anyway. You lied

about telling the truth. My dad—" he flicked his hand out toward the empty street; his voice cracked "—said he wanted me…wanted us to be a family."

"Seth, your dad lied about many things, but I can't imagine him not wanting you."

A slow drizzle left spots on the shoulders of Seth's fleece jacket. After pulling the hood over his head, the lanky eleven-year-old wrapped his arms around himself, becoming a small ball of gray.

"He said it was my fault. He wasn't the one who wanted kids while he was still in college. He said me and Mom ruined his life."

Jake couldn't stand it any longer. He put his hand on the thin shoulder and pulled Seth against him. "You're Vickie's pride and joy. In addition, your grandparents can't stop bragging about you. And even if everyone in your family lets you down, you still belong to God. He has always wanted you."

A few people came out to get in their cars, laughing at the rain. Seth stepped back, and Jake waved, giving them a tight smile.

Once their taillights vanished in the shadows, he stepped closer to Seth again. "You were not an accident or mistake. God knew you and loved you before your parents ever came together."

Seth buried his face farther into his hood. "But I thought God said to honor our parents?" He took a breath then looked up at Jake, his eyes large between long wisps of blond hair, the same color of his mother's. "He got mad when I wouldn't help him get Papa Jack's account passwords. He said I was useless and locked the car doors. He wouldn't let me in his car." His words were broken by hiccups.

How could people treat their children with such callousness? "I'm so sorry, Seth. Unfortunately, people, fathers, will disappoint us. God is the only perfect Father. We might turn our backs to Him, but He never leaves us."

"Was God with you when you killed your father?"

Jake had never thought about it before. He let his mind go back to that night again, the fear for his family so overwhelming he hadn't thought about anything else. He now remembered his mother praying; her prayers had only made her husband more violent.

The mist had turned into a soft rain. Jake wiped the wetness off his face.

Light poured out from the side door. "Seth!" Vickie's worried voice carried clear and loud across the parking lot.

"We're over here." With his hand on Seth's back he guided him toward the door where Vickie stood. The warm light from inside surrounded her body, creating a silhouette. She stepped out of the doorway meeting them halfway.

"Is everything all right?" She pushed Seth's hair back from his eyes. "When I couldn't find you, I got worried."

"I'm okay, Mom." He stuffed his hands in his front pockets. "I followed Dad out. He left. I think it might be for good." He glanced at Jake. "Will you answer my question?"

"Question?"

"Was God with you when you shot your father?"

"Seth!" Vickie whispered.

"No, it's okay." Seeing Vickie had distracted him, and for a moment, he forgot about the question Seth had asked him. "Yeah, He was there, even though my father ranted at Him and us. God was there in the storm of my father's rage. He stayed with me. He's the reason I know I can be my own man, a man of God. I don't have to make my father's choices."

Vickie pulled Seth against her, hugging him tight. "After what happened, how did you know to look for God?" She whispered her own question.

He frowned. How did he know? "My mom, I guess. The police that came to the house kept us outside. One of them brought us each a bag of our clothes and gave us a place to go for families in crisis. They even called to make sure they had room for us. That's when one of the officers gave Esmi her teddy bear."

He paused, collecting his thoughts from the aftermath of that night. "My mother pointed out there were men of honor, but ultimately God was our true Father and I should live for Him every day of my life. She told me that almost every day for that first year. I also had other role models in my life, like J.W."

"Is that why you became a state trooper?" Seth asked.

Jake smiled. "Yeah, I think so. I like the idea of protecting people like my mother."

Vickie squeezed Seth closer to her side. "Your mother is a very special woman."

"I'm blessed to have some amazing women in my life. So are you, Seth."

Thunder rumbled, and a flash of lightning dispensed all the shadows for a second. He studied her features for any sign of the disgust he saw earlier and couldn't find a trace. Maybe optimism wouldn't be misplaced.

She reached across the space and pushed back some of his hair that the shower had plastered to his forehead. She whispered, "It's like God is crying for you."

Hitting his chest, his heart reached back to her. His grin grew; yes, there was hope. "Vickie Lawson, you are more sentimental than you let on to the good people of Clear Water."

"Shh, don't tell anyone." She looked down to her son. "Are you two ready to go in? I think it might actually rain this time."

Walking back into the building, Jake found his mother in the midst of a vicious group of warrior women. When they all turned to him, he hesitated.

His mother stepped out and grabbed his hand.

"Oh, *mijo*, I'm so sorry. I thought it best never to talk about it. Not once did I dream of this happening."

He kissed the side of her head as he hugged her close, the comforting smell of rose and vanilla washed through his senses. "We did the best we could with what we were given. No worries, okay?" He whispered against her hair.

She pulled away and patted his cheek. "I think you deserve some of your favorite cookies." She turned and headed for the kitchen area.

He tried to follow but as people were leaving, they kept stopping him to talk. Wasn't it about time for everyone to go home? He smiled and thanked them for their support.

Finally arriving in the kitchen, Jake found his mother cupping Vickie's mother's hands in both of her worn palms.

"Mrs. Lawson, I'm so sorry, I…"

"You don't owe her an apology, Mother." He looked at the woman who had thought he wasn't good enough for her daughter. He sighed. Of course, he had believed it also.

Maria put her hand on his chest. "*Mijo*, I moved into their house without telling them the truth."

"I have always supported your mother. Everything we do is for our children, good or bad. I can't imagine having to protect my children from their own father." Elizabeth Lawson glanced to her own daughter. "I don't need an apology from your mother. I'm awed with her strength."

J.W. joined them, Seth under his arm. "Hey, Lizzy bug, you ready to head out? I told Vickie we'd take the kiddos home with us."

Jake shook his head and grinned. Only J.W. got away with calling Elizabeth Marie Lawson by a silly nickname. It somehow made her more human. Then he sobered, thinking of the morning this man he greatly respected had asked him to run for sheriff. "Sir, don't worry about me asking for you to support me for sheriff. I doubt I'll be running."

"Hogwash! I knew all about this before your mother took the job. Well, not the part about you actually doing the shooting, but I knew the story. It was one of the reasons I hired her." He smiled at Maria. "Those nine years were the best eating I ever had at my table." He winked at Maria before pulling his wife into a side hug.

"Jackson Walker, behave." Elizabeth shook her head, and with a roll of her eyes, she patted his arm.

Jake's mind shot back to the words J.W. had so casually spoken. "You knew?" His voice rising a bit higher than he intended.

Vickie walked up. "Who knew what?"

"Papa Jack knew that Jake's dad beat them up and they shot him." Seth had summed up the story.

"Daddy, you knew about this and never said anything?"

"Wasn't my story to tell." He held eye contact

with Jake. "Stephen Randall, a business associate from Eagle Pass, had called me earlier that week. Lizzy had mentioned at a dinner that we needed a new housekeeper and cook. They said their house-keeper, Maria, was looking to move because of her husband and they wanted to help her."

"You had made plans to leave?" This was the first time Jake had heard about this. That explained the escalation of his father's violence.

Lips tight, she nodded, looking uncomfortable talking about her past. "You were getting bigger and had started challenging him. He didn't like being confronted. I had to get you and Esmi out but didn't know how, so I started asking Mrs. Randall about other jobs far away."

"Linda had called Elizabeth earlier about Maria, but that night we put the plans in fast forward and had y'all moved in by the end of the week."

"I had prayed for God to give us a safe place to go. He sent us here." His mother wrapped her arm around his. "I told you God would take care of us."

Elizabeth smiled. "God is amazing."

Jake hated to admit it, but he looked at Vickie's mother in a new light.

Lupe hugged Maria. "I'm so glad. I just wished you had felt safe enough to talk to me."

"Oh, that wasn't it. I just wanted to forget the past and not think about the horrible night." She glanced at Jake. "I thought not talking about it would make it easier to move on."

"Maria's coming home with me. We want to get started on a business plan," Lupe said.

"Me, an independent businesswoman." Maria's voice carried threads of amazement at the thought.

Pride swelled. Jake hugged her again. Not only had they survived, they flourished. He sent a quick thanks to God.

"We're taking the kids home." Elizabeth gathered her dishes. "Jake, could you bring Vickie? She needs to pick up her car at our house."

Well, that was new. He cut a glance to Vickie with brows raised. She shrugged back, with a nod.

"I'll make sure she gets home."

"Good." With a kiss on her daughter's cheek, Mrs. Lawson herded her husband and grandkids out the door.

Maria gave him a last hug and patted his face. "God is good in everything. Sometimes we forget." She gave Vickie a fast hug also. "I'm sure I'll see you later."

Jake leaned back against the counter. Alone finally, but he didn't know how to start. The door opened. Relief clashed with frustration on his already tight nerves. Pastor John and a small group of elders came into the room.

The deacons smiled and nodded toward Jake as the group settled around one of the tables. Pastor John made his way over to Jake and Vickie. "Sorry, I didn't realize you were still in here." He smiled at Vickie before turning to Jake. "You okay?"

"Yeah, I'm good. I'm sorry about the drama. Thanks for supporting me without knowing all the truth. It means a lot to me."

"Anytime. God is always good. Sometimes it can be hard to trust Him with our whole life. Especially the parts we want to keep hidden." He tossed a hard candy in his mouth. "If y'all need to talk, the sanctuary's open. You're more than welcome to use it."

"Thanks, we'll let you get back to your meeting." Jake placed his hand on Vickie's back as he guided her across the room and walked down the carpeted hall to the back doors of the sanctuary. He still needed to talk to her about Tommy.

# *Chapter Nineteen*

Anticipation crawled across her skin. The warmth of his hand anchored her in the present. He paused to open the heavy wood door behind the baptismal font. Following him to the front pew, Vickie wondered if she was ready to be the woman he needed.

This could be it. Did they have a future together? Could they find a way to make it real?

"Vickie." He pulled her down to the pew next to him. "I want you to know I put a great deal of thought into this. It was not something I did lightly." He took a deep breath and looked away from her.

Her heart rate increased as she sat on the edge of the cushioned bench. His fingers entwined with hers like the deep roots of the old cypress trees along the river.

*Sit still and be quiet.* Vickie forced herself to listen, no interruptions or assumptions. She understood his hesitation, after so many years of denying their feelings. This was scary territory, building their own roots.

"I called a friend in Florida to do a little fact finding for me." Jake ran his fingers through his damp hair then looked back at her. "Tommy's in trouble. Deep, financial trouble. If the rumor is correct, it's the kind that can lead to breaking laws or getting him killed."

"What?" She blinked, recalibrating her thoughts. He wanted to talk about Tommy?

"What worries me the most is he asked Seth for your father's passwords. My guess? He thought to sweep in, remarry you and get access to your family's money. When you blocked him, he planned to steal it, using Seth. He's desperate, Vickie. I'm not sure you're safe right now."

"He asked Seth to help him embezzle Daddy's accounts?" She pulled her hand out of Jake's and rubbed her face. She didn't want to hear this. "Why didn't you tell me sooner?" *Breathe, Vickie. Slow down and breathe.* "Okay, Tommy's a liar and a manipulator, but he wouldn't physically hurt us." She looked into Jake's dark eyes, searching for answers. "Would he?"

"Vickie, I think maybe you should move in with your parents for now, until we get this cleared up."

"No, I've worked too hard to go backward. You can't just start telling me what to do." She stood, walking to the stained-glass window. Running her hand along the brass plate, she thought of her father. Without looking, she knew what the grooves spelled out. *In Loving Memory of Jackson Walker Lawson III and Mabel Marie Lawson.* Her grandparents.

She turned, resting her hands behind her on the ledge. "I didn't come back to hide behind Daddy. I'll talk to him, but I'm not living in his house again. Can I get a restraining order on Tommy?"

"Sure, but it's just a piece of paper. It won't stop him if he wants something from you." He walked to the window next to her and braced himself on his fist. "I have a small cottage I built for my mother. She never…"

"No!" Waving her hand at him, she said, "I'm not living on your property, either."

"Vickie, don't be stubborn. Let me help you. You could rent it from me if that makes you feel better." He stood, reaching for her hand. Jake wrapped his fingers around hers and pulled her to him. "You're right when you said I ran when I should have talked to you. I feared turning into my father. If something happened to you or the kids, I'd never forgive myself. Let me help you."

"Jake, this is not about your father. I don't want to be another rescue project. I need to know I can take care of my family."

"I understand, but being strong doesn't mean you have to do everything alone. You can rent the cottage from me. It only has two rooms and one bath, but the kitchen and living room are large, bigger than the trailer. You can pay me whatever amount you're giving your dad."

"Let me think about it."

"I don't know if we have time. If Tommy is up against a wall, he's dangerous." He took her restless fingers in his hand and held them still.

With a long heavy sigh, she shook her head. "A couple more weeks won't matter."

He closed his eyes and groaned. "Stubborn." Opening his eyes, he leaned into her, less than an inch separated their noses. "You promise to call me or your dad the minute Tommy pulls into your drive. Tell the kids not to go with him." He cupped her face in his hands. "Being independent is fine, but don't put yourself or the kids at risk because of some false pride. Promise you'll call."

She nodded. "I'll call, and I'll have your number posted by the phone. Can you take me home now? I really want to see my kids."

"Come on." With his fingers still entwined with hers, he led her to the double doors of the sanctuary. He opened the heavy oak entry and led her through.

The drizzle turned to rain as they hurried across the lawn to his truck. His hand on her waist, he helped lift her up into the seat.

Making his way to the driver's side, he pushed the rain-soaked hair off his forehead. Climbing in next to her, he grinned. "Praise the Lord for the rain."

Joy simmered through her whole body, causing

a laugh to escape. "Daddy always said he'd rather deal with a flood than a drought."

"I enjoy a good rain, but as a state trooper I'm not sure I'd agree about the flood. Of course, fires can be brutal, too."

A brilliant flash of lightning lit up the sky. She shrieked, and Jake laughed at her. Placing her hand over her heart, she joined him. She had always loved the rain and thunder, but all that electrical force frightened her.

"Sorry, I hate when I yell like that." She looked out the window, but everything had gone dark again.

"Don't worry about it. You can yell at the lightning all you want."

He always accepted her, flaws and all. She wanted to scoot over and sit right next to him, but she stayed on her side of the cab.

Grinning, she could imagine Jake scolding her to get back in her seat belt. For him, safety always came first.

She looked out the window, not seeing the familiar sights through the heavy rain and darkness. Vickie needed a bit of distance between them, anyway.

Walking disaster pretty much summed up her life right now. She needed to clean up her mess, and then maybe she could look to a future with Jake.

Unable to resist the urge to touch him she reached

across the back of the seat and rested her hand on his shoulder.

"I'm scared, Jake." What she wasn't sure of was if it was Tommy that put her nerves on edge or being so close to Jake and losing the chance for a future with him again.

"Time and time again I've seen God work in my life and yours. Don't let fear stop you from living on faith." He patted her hand, never taking his focus off the road ahead. "I can escort you and the kids to church in the morning."

"That sounds good." She realized he had known it wasn't the lightning that really scared her but choices she needed to make.

She took a minute to picture them all sitting in a pew. Tommy had only gone to church because it looked good for his political career. How did she ever pick him over Jake?

The sky opened up, and the rain hit the windshield so hard the headlights couldn't penetrate the curtain of water.

Jake eased off the accelerator. He stayed focused on the tempest outside their protected shell. Both hands firmly gripped the leather wheel, guiding them through the storm.

It took them twice the time it normally did to get to her parents' house. Pulling around the circular drive, Jake parked as close to the entry as possible. Cutting the engine, he peered out the window.

"It's let up a little, but I think we're going to have to make a run for it."

"I promise I won't melt." She started pushing on the door.

"Wait. I'll come around and we can run under my jacket."

"Okay." She smiled. Maybe it was wrong, but she liked the idea of being close to him, sharing his coat.

With one hand on the hood, and the other holding the jacket over his head, he ran to her side. When he opened the door, she jumped down and took his hand. Moving his hand up her arm, he pulled her along, rushing to her parents' front porch.

A memory stopped her feet from moving forward. He glanced at her, his forehead wrinkled. "What's wrong?" His gaze slid down to her feet before coming back up, fixing his eyes on her face.

She swallowed. Should she share her old daydream with him? Huddled under his jacket, the rain still drenched them. Her fingers rose to his face. Water drops hung on his black lashes. For a moment, she lost all thought as his rich, dark eyes stared at her. Questioning. Anyone who found brown boring had never looked into the depth of color in Jake's eyes.

"Victoria?"

"I always imagined what it would be like to kiss you." Her gaze moved from his eyes to the pout of his full lips. "Twice we've come close." She smiled at him. "I think the third time might be the one we get right. I used to dream of kissing you in the rain."

Moving her other hand to his jaw, she cupped the face she loved. Vickie almost reached his lips and then stopped, unsure.

"You're crazy, you know that?" He smiled as if he liked crazy.

Vickie laughed and ran her finger down his neck. His pulse made her feel alive.

He wrapped his arms around her, lifting her up until their lips made contact. His coat slipped to the ground as both of his arms pulled her close. The softness of his lips connected to every nerve in her body. He took his time exploring the contour of her mouth. He made her feel cherished and loved.

Leaving her lips, he whispered against her ear. "How was that?"

Her lungs forgot how to work. She managed to murmur, "Shattered my expectations."

"I'd love to continue this experiment of yours, but I think we might be gaining an audience." He tilted his head to the big picture window.

She'd gotten so caught up in the moment, she'd forgot she was outside her parents' house. Heat climbed up her neck.

He laughed, grabbed his coat and her hand and started running to the porch, dragging her along. "Girl, you take me back to high school."

"You mean the way high school should've been?"

Standing under the porch, he shook his head, throwing water in all directions. In response, she did the same until they both laughed so hard she had tears in her eyes.

The door open, her mother stood with one perfectly shaped eyebrow arched.

Jake coughed and straightened his spine. "Mrs. Lawson, we finally got some rain." He gave a polite nod to Vickie. "I'll see you in the morning. Around 9:30?"

"Make it nine, and you can eat breakfast with us."

"Both of you, stop this chitchat and come inside. You need to dry off before you get sick."

"Yes, Momma." She grabbed his hand. "Come on."

Jake hesitated, looking from her hand to the front door. She realized he had always entered the house through the kitchen. Vickie stepped closer to him. "It's like an alternate universe, isn't it?"

He grinned and squeezed her hand. The words didn't have to be spoken. They were about to walk into her parents' house hand in hand.

# *Chapter Twenty*

The next morning, Vickie woke up to a new day and a new future. Jake promised to take her to church. She couldn't stop smiling. With Tommy gone, she could focus on her tomorrows.

"Rise and shine!" Vickie sang loud and off-key. She'd always loved Sunday mornings. She heard Seth groan.

Poking her head in his room, she found him under his pillow. "How about pancakes this morning?"

Ashley jumped into the hallway with a smile on her face, always ready to start a new day. "Can I have mouse ears on my pancakes?"

"That's a great idea. Go on in the bathroom and start getting ready." She walked over to her son's bed and pulled the pillow off his head. "You have fifteen minutes then it's your turn in the bathroom. Jake's joining us for breakfast." She started to close the door behind her.

"Mom?" He sat up in his bed, the nightshirt tight across his shoulders and his hair sticking up in different directions.

She stopped and looked at her boy turning teenager. "Yeah?"

He rubbed his eyes before looking back at her. "Are you and Jake going to date?"

She stepped into the room with a sigh. Everything she did affected her children. "Well, we might decide to spend more time together. I'm not sure at this point what is going to happen."

A deep frown pulled on his face. "What does that mean?"

Good question. She moved closer, stepping over some unidentified object and sat on the foot of his bed. "We really like each other. We were best friends growing up." She bit her bottom lip. "How do you feel about Jake and me being together?"

"He's a good guy, I guess. I think he really likes you." He turned to her. "He makes you laugh. I like it when you laugh."

"Seth, if you…have questions or get upset, please, talk to me or at least to someone you can trust like Pastor John."

His eyes went big. "Rachel's dad?"

"Yes, he is our pastor." She couldn't resist pushing some of his hair into place. "You also have Papa Jack. Who else would you talk to?"

"Officer Torres. I know I got mad last night, but

he still listened to me and answered my questions. Mom, why is Dad so mean sometimes?"

She pushed his bed-tousled hair back. "Your father's very complicated. He worked hard at being successful. How other people see him is important, and he…he thinks money and popularity will make him happy."

"Papa Jack said he's lost and I shouldn't listen to him."

"Oh, Seth, I think you father is confused about his purpose and he is hurting the people that he should be loving. We could pray for him."

"Can we?"

She nodded and held her hand out, waiting for him to take it. "Dear God, Father in heaven. We come to You with open hearts asking for You to watch over Tommy and let him know how much You, Seth and Ashley love him." She squeezed his fingers. "Do you want to add anything?"

"We pray that my father finds You. Thank You for bringing us to Clear Water. Watch over Papa Jack and Grandma. And God, please bring happiness to Mama's life. Amen."

"Amen." She kept her head down a couple of heartbeats before standing. "I'm going to get the batter started." She leaned forward and kissed his forehead. "I love you, Seth, and nothing will ever change that. You will always be my treasure."

In the kitchen, Vickie turned on the radio and started dancing as she flipped on the coffeemaker and gathered everything for the pancake feast. She heard a car door slam and stopped humming.

*Oh, no.* Her hands fluttered over her hair. Jake was early, and she looked a fright. Ashley walked in dressed in her favorite yellow-and-green-flowered dress with the pink cowboy boots. Her fashion choices would have to be fixed later.

"Sweetheart, I think Jake just pulled up. I'm going to run to my bedroom and change." As she moved to her room behind the kitchen, she kept giving orders. "Have him sit down, and get him something to drink. I'll be right out."

"Okay, Mommy."

With her door closed, Vickie leaned against it and suppressed the urge to giggle. Her gaze darted to her closet. No idea what to wear. *Come on, girl, this is Sunday morning worship, not the prom.*

She twisted her hair high and clipped it on her head, letting the curls fall. A quick swipe of makeup to add some light color. Next she hurried to the closet. The turquoise tunic would be a good color, maybe with the brown skirt.

Standing in front of the mirror, she bit her bottom lip. Not perfect, but she heard voices down the hall, so she didn't give herself more time to doubt her selection.

Vickie opened the door. No giggling.

Reaching the kitchen, she froze.

"Mommy, look! Daddy wants to go to church with us."

Instead of Jake, Tommy sat at the counter.

He smiled with his hand over Ashley's small shoulders, "Hello, Vic."

"What are you doing here?" Her muscles coiled and flexed.

"I told you I'm not leaving without my family." He ruffled Ashley's hair.

She hadn't time to explain the new rules about Tommy with Ashley. Seth stood in the hallway, a cell phone in his hand. She gave him a smile and nodded.

Hopefully, the smile wasn't as tight as it felt. He glanced at his dad then looked down again. He sent the text. To Jake, if he stuck to the plan. Maybe she was being paranoid after Jake had them plan for a worst-case scenario with her parents.

She glanced at Ashley. "Sweetheart, your Bible's in my room. Let's go get it, okay?"

Ashley hopped down from the tall stool. "Mommy reads from it at night before I go to sleep."

Once in the room, she closed the door. "Here is my cell. I need you to call Papa Jack to come pick you up. Tell him your dad's here. Lock the door behind me and stay in here until Papa Jack or Jake arrives. No one else."

"Why?"

"Just do it, promise?"

"Okay." A frown creased her sweet face.

This time Vickie prepared herself for seeing her

ex-husband in her house. One step out the door and she paused, waiting to hear the click. She prayed while making her way through the washroom and into the kitchen. "Tommy, I told you not to come by unless you called first."

"That's stupid, Vic. I'm your husband. How can we get our family back together if I can't prove to you I've changed? Come on, give me another chance." He took a sip of the orange juice Ashley had poured for him. "You said I owed Seth an apology. That's why I'm here."

She glanced around, making sure Seth had gone to his room. "You've had plenty of chances." She wondered how much to tell him she knew of Florida. Stomach in a knot, she dove in all the way. "You could have talked to him last night, but instead you locked him out of your car. We are finished, Tommy. You might as well go back to Florida."

He stood. Coming closer to her, he reached out and ran his fingertips up her arm. "I was on the phone with a business partner. I didn't realize he was there. Man, that drama about Jake was shocking."

She stepped away from him.

"Come on, Vic. We have everything waiting for us, but it's nothing without you. I miss you and the kids so much. I just want my family back."

She moved out of his reach. "Really? I hear you need some money."

"That's a lie." He followed her. "Who told you that? Your little boyfriend, Torres? After his past came bubbling up, he's looking for a way to make me out to be the bad guy. He's the one that lied to everybody."

"I'm not talking about Jake. Even if I went to Florida with you, we still wouldn't have any money."

"Your daddy would give it to you if you asked. He owes me, anyway. We lost everything because he refused to publicly endorse me for senator."

Outrage rushed the blood to her heart. "Daddy doesn't owe you anything. He paid for your law degree."

"Only after you got pregnant. You were always messing up my plans." He moved into her space, backing her into the refrigerator door. "But we both know he'll do anything for his grandkids." He pulled a handgun from his jacket. "I'm not leaving until we come to an understanding."

The word *fear* took on a new definition as all of the blood fled Vickie's legs. He would really hurt them. She closed her eyes for a quick prayer to give her wisdom.

She had to keep him calm until Jake or her dad got here. "Please, Tommy, you don't need a gun. We can talk about this. Please don't scare the kids." How was she ever fooled into thinking she could love this man?

He stepped back and turned to the living room,

pacing like a big cat in a small cage. He laid the gun on the counter and ran shaking fingers through his hair. "Vic, you don't understand. I don't want to hurt you or the kids, but I'm running out of options and with one check your father could fix all our problems."

"Let me call my daddy. You're right, he can help us." Or get hurt trying to help us. *Oh, God, please, please give me the words to get us out of here safely.* Her lungs and heart felt too big for her rib cage.

Tommy swung his arm and knocked the lamp off the end table. "You're lying. Your father won't help me." With a lunge, he turned back to her. "I'm out of time. What are your father's account numbers?" He pinned her against the green door of the freezer.

She shook her head. "I don't know." She closed her eyes, letting God give her a peace only He could. "Tommy, we can figure something out."

"You don't understand." He put his face less than an inch from her ear and said, "I'm not letting you destroy my life again." He slammed her head back on the hard surface behind her. A burst of stars blocked her vision.

"Stop." Seth's frantic voice came from the living room. "Let her go."

All the blood rushed out of her so fast, her joints went numb. Tommy's arm kept her standing on hollow legs. She had told Seth to stay in his bedroom.

Her throat started burning. Seth was not supposed to be in here.

"Stay out of this!" Tommy yelled.

In a blur of motion, Tommy moved away from her. Vickie stumbled forward. She heard a thump. Shaking her head to clear her vision, she found Tommy holding Seth. The phone at his feet. "No!" She had to get Tommy's attention back on her. "He doesn't know anything."

She reached for Tommy's arm as he raised it to strike Seth, but it wasn't enough. To stop him, she threw her whole body into his larger frame.

Tommy twisted around and grabbed her. He heaved her backward, the base of her spine hitting the edge of the counter.

He lunged at her, and his fingers wrapped around her throat.

Instinctively, her hands went to his wrist as he shook her. Lungs begged for air as she forced her brain to think.

With her left hand, she reached for the coffee-pot. Her fingers missed the handle, but she ignored the burn and threw the hot liquid at Tommy's face.

He screamed, jumping back from her.

Her hand started to burn. "Get outside, Seth, run."

Tommy yanked her by the hair and threw her into the coffee table. The impact of her body shattered the fragile piece of cheap furniture.

"You don't understand, Vickie," he yelled over her. "I don't want to hurt you, but I have to get that money. They'll ruin me."

"Tommy, you don't want to do this." She pulled herself up, crawling backward until her shoulders hit the sofa. She needed to slow him down. "I don't have access to any money, but I can get it if you let me call Daddy."

He kept moving forward. "I'll take the kids to Florida. I'm their father. If J.W. wants his grandkids, he'll pay me." Red welts appeared across his cheek and neck. He sat on his heels. "Where's Ashley?" He stood and looked toward her bedroom door.

His now calm voice terrified her. If she could just keep his focus on her, Jake or her dad would be here and the kids would be safe.

Her head hurt, her back hurt, maybe it would be easier if she focused on the part of her body that didn't hurt. Her left hand seemed fine. She pointed her good hand at him, clenching her teeth.

She looked him in the eye. "You. Are. Not. Taking. My. Children."

"What's your dad's account and password? I know you have access to at least one in case of an emergency. All you have to do is give it to me." He shook her.

If she could hang on, keep him focused on her, Jake or her father would be here soon.

"Stop!" A voice broke through the haze. She wanted to weep. Seth hadn't left. "Leave her alone!"

Tommy let go.

"No." Her world stopped spinning. Forcing her eyes open, she found Seth in front of her, legs apart, the gun Tommy had brought into the house now pointed at the man that should have protected them.

On the other side of the small room Tommy stood with one of the jagged-tipped legs of the broken table in his hand, holding it like a club. He took a step forward.

Vickie tried to stand; she had to stop this, had to get Seth out of this house. "Seth, no."

Tommy laughed. "Son, you don't have the guts to shoot me." He took another step toward them.

Jake whistled as he turned off the Farm to Market road and headed to Vickie's house. With the downpour from last night, the landscape already looked more alive.

Life was good.

Then he saw Tommy's Mercedes-Benz next to the little Ford Focus. Without slowing, he made a sharp turn through the gate.

Dust flew behind him as he slammed his truck into Park. He took a deep breath, calming himself down.

He had to compartmentalize his thoughts. He

didn't know the situation, and the last thing they needed was him barging in and overreacting.

He pulled his gun and stepped out of his truck. Before he reached the new steps he heard a gunshot.

# Chapter Twenty-One

Running to the front door, Jake paused with his hand on the knob and his shoulder pressed against the rough surface.

His instinct wanted him to burst in and make sure Vickie and the kids remained unharmed.

Taking a deep breath, he listened for any clues about the circumstances on the other side of the door.

"I told you not to move." Seth's voice shook. Relief flooded Jake's system for a moment. The kid must be the one with the gun.

Sweat beaded on his upper lip. Jake wasn't sure if that was good or bad. Flashes of his own childhood nightmare flew across his brain. What brought Seth to the point of pulling a gun on his father?

Easing the door open, he slipped into the room and slowly scanned the scene. Vickie stood with her hands on Seth's shoulders. He couldn't see her face behind a mess of hair. Gripped tightly in Seth's hands was a handgun, pointed at his dad. The coffee table was in pieces on the floor along with a lamp.

Tommy faced the mother-and-son team, the color gone from his face, making the red welts that splashed across his cheek and neck shine in contrast. In his hand was the jagged end of a broken table leg.

Looking past Tommy, he found where the bullet had made its exit, right through the family picture, taking out Tommy's face.

He didn't see Ashley. He took one step forward, ready to take down Tommy if he needed to. "Tommy, put down the weapon."

Tommy glanced down and looked surprised to see the wood leg in his hand. He dropped it.

"Seth, I need you to lower your weapon."

"He hit…he hit Mama, threw her across the room."

"Seth. You've done a great job protecting her. I need you to step down and lower the weapon."

Vickie rubbed her arms. She whispered in Seth's ear. Not taking his eyes off his father, Seth lowered the gun. With slow motions, Jake took it out of his hands. Dropping the ammo out of the chamber, Jake finally took a breath.

"Where is Ashley?" He couldn't breathe until he knew they were all safe.

Vickie wrapped her arms around Seth. "She's in my bedroom. Oh, she must be scared."

"Mom, you're bleeding!"

Wiping at her face with her sleeve, she reassured her son. "I'm okay."

Tommy started moving toward them. "I didn't mean to hurt you."

Jake took a step in front of them, his weight balanced on his front leg, ready to attack if Tommy made any suspicious moves. Jake acknowledged a part of him really want to take Tommy down, but he needed to stay on the logical side of his brain right now. Keeping his weapon trained on Tommy, Jake took a moment to assure himself everyone was fine.

"Tommy, you are going to stay right there until the sheriff gets here." He took a deep breath. "Seth, take your mother to her room and help her clean up. Wait, do you have a camera?"

Tommy took another step. "She doesn't need a camera. It was all a misunderstanding, an accident. Right, Vickie?"

"Tommy, I said, don't move."

"Mom?"

Vickie pushed her hair back and looked straight at Tommy. "There is no misunderstanding. You asked for my father's money and I said no, so you beat me up."

"I'm the one that got hot coffee in the face and my own son shot at me." He sneered at Jake. "Maybe I'll press charges."

Seth straightened, his slim body shaking. "You

hit her then threw her across the room like she was nothin'!" Moisture hung on his lashes as he swallowed. His young voice broke.

Jake rested his hand on the boy's trembling shoulder, feeling all the pain of watching a woman you love being beaten and you were too weak to stop it. "Seth, you did well. You protected your family and didn't even hurt anyone." He glanced over at Vickie. Everything on the inside froze. His heart and lungs stopped working. Behind her mass of curls, she had hidden a crushed and bloodied face.

He turned to Tommy. "Seth, I'm proud of you. Take your mother to her room after a couple of pictures and help her clean up. I'll take care of Tommy."

"Jake?" Vickie's whispered voice calmed the heat rising in his veins, a little bit.

"Vickie, go with Seth. You don't want your parents to see you like this."

She laid her hand on his arm. "Jake, be smart."

"Come on, Mom. Ashley's probably scared." Her son led her through the kitchen to her room.

Silence shrouded the destroyed living room as the men stared at each other. Jake didn't trust his self-control enough to talk. In the distance, sirens could be heard. He also heard a diesel truck in the drive. That would be J.W.

"Torres, this is ridiculous. We both know how hotheaded Vickie can be when she's upset. It just got a little out of control."

Jake narrowed his eyes and planted his feet, otherwise he might show Tommy boy just how out of control he could get.

"I don't know why I'm even trying to talk to you. I'm leaving."

Jake blocked his path to the door. "We're waiting for the sheriff, and I believe J.W. just pulled up." He saw Tommy glance to the door, sweat beading up across his upper lip. "Don't give me the excuse to tackle you. We both know I can. If I accidently hit you a few times we'll just call it a misunderstanding."

"Knowing your background, I guess I'm lucky you didn't tell the boy to shoot me."

"I think Seth made it clear where you stand in the family." He nodded to the family portrait now hanging crooked on the wall. The right corner was gone, the area where Tommy's face had been. Now Vickie alone sat with her children around her.

For the first time since seeing the black Mercedes-Benz, Jake smiled. Yes, he was proud of Seth. *Thank You, God, for keeping them safe and providing all they needed to be strong through You.*

Taking a few steps backward, he made room for J.W. as he barged through the door.

Vickie stood between Jake and her father as they watched the sheriff's car disappear down the road. Tommy sat handcuffed in the backseat. Apparently, because he brought the gun into the house, the charges would be harsher, even though Seth had pulled the trigger. She had pulled her hair in a ponytail and changed out of her church clothes. She now wore her favorite T-shirt and jeans. She still felt like she needed a long soak in a mountain of bubbles.

The image of her son holding a gun played over and over in her head.

She was horrified that her son witnessed such a violent scene between his parents, but so proud of him at the same time. He had made the choice to shoot at the picture of his dad instead of shooting the man.

Her father had been taking Seth to gun safety classes. She reached for her father's hand and squeezed it, wincing in pain.

Seth had told the sheriff how he shot the warning because Papa Jack had been taking him to the practice range and he remembered what Jake had told him about his own father.

"Thanks, Daddy, for keeping the kids busy while I talked to the sheriff."

"I'd better hurry back home before your mother makes her way over here." He turned to Jake. "You'll be staying for a while, right?"

Vickie shook her head at the silent communication between her father and Jake. J.W. pulled Vickie into his arms, hugging her tight against his chest, but then quickly released her when she tried to muffle cries of pain.

"Vickie, I love you." He patted her back a couple of times before stepping away. "I promised your mother that you would be at our house as soon I could get you there." He turned to Jake. "She expects you there for dinner, too."

"Yes, sir."

"Might as well pack a few things. I don't think she's letting you out of her sight once she hears the whole story."

"Okay. I don't think I could sleep here, anyway." She hugged him close this time, taking in the smell of his aftershave. "I love you more than the world is round, Daddy."

He squeezed back. "Love you to the moon and back, girl of mine. Call if you need anything." He headed to his truck.

She tried to stand straight and look confident, but judging by the pity in Jake's eyes she hadn't pulled it off. "Tommy got here before breakfast, so the kids haven't eaten. You haven't, either. Come in, I'll fix the pancakes."

She paused at the top of the steps and smiled back at him. "I think of you every time I walk to my door. You're so good at making things better."

"I wish I could have built a way to keep him out, or at least been here when he walked into your house."

"He would have found another way to get to me. He could've grabbed the kids from school. No one would have stopped him. In a way this was good."

She ran her hand over the smooth railing. "I can't get the image of Seth holding the gun out of my head." She tried to stop the sob from escaping. "Then I see you as a little boy pulling the trigger. Oh, Jake, children should be safe from this horror. To fight the very people who should love and protect you is wrong." She covered her face with her hands.

Jake came up the last steps and pulled her into his arms, her head pressed against his shirt.

She gripped his upper arms and started to cry. Her body hurt, but Jake relieved the pain in her heart. With him it was okay to cry, just for a little bit.

Finished, she stepped back and patted her face dry. "Sorry."

He put the side of his knuckle under her chin. "I thought we already agreed you would not apologize for your emotions."

She leaned back in his arms and studied her own personal hero. Tracing his jaw with her good hand, she followed along the edge until she stopped at his chin. Her gaze moved to his lips.

Standing on her toes, she tilted her head up. Fingers now entwined in his thick hair, she pulled him down.

The sweetest touch of their lips followed before he stepped back.

She longed to say the words. They hovered on her tongue. She blinked. Fear stopped her.

She had said them before with Tommy. The words had no meaning. They ended up hollow. Taking a step back, she smiled at Jake. He deserved the words, but she couldn't do it, not now.

"Ready for some pancakes?" Not what she wanted to say, nor could she imagine eating right now, but it would keep him in her universe a bit longer.

"Sounds good." He followed her into the house. She left him picking up pieces of shattered coffee table as she made her way to her room.

Hesitant to face her children's questions, she slowly entered her room. Pausing, she drank in the sight of Seth propped against her headboard. Ashley tucked under one arm while he read to her.

"Mommy!" Her daughter saw her first and jumped up. Vickie almost lost her balance as the force of the small body slammed into her. "Seth was reading stories from my Bible."

"Is everything okay?" The concern on her son's face broke her heart.

"It is now. How about I fix those pancakes and we can talk about it?"

"Sounds good, Mom. Is Jake still here?"

"Yes. He's in the living room." She picked up Ashley and hugged her close. Her daughter's small hands cupped her face.

"Why did Daddy hurt you?"

A lump of excuses clogged her throat.

Seth put his hand on his sister's back. "I told her

Dad's lost and confused. His anger has nothing to do with us." He looked at Vickie. "Right, Mom?"

She nodded, pulled him close and kissed the top of his head. "I love you both so much. Come on, let's go make some mouse-eared pancakes."

As she entered the kitchen, Ashley slid down her hip and went to Jake. "What happened to the table?"

He had made a pile of the broken wood pieces by the door.

Seth spoke up first. "Mom and Dad got in a fight, and the table got in the way."

A frown filled Ashley's face. She stood over the broken table, her small hands fisted on her hips. "I don't think it can be fixed."

Jake held two pieces in his hand. "There is not a glue in the world strong enough to put this old thing back together again."

Vickie toed the shattered edge of the top. "It was fake, anyway."

Jake started picking up more broken fragments. "Hey, guys, you want to help me haul this to the burn pit while your mom makes those pancakes?"

"We can burn it? Yay! I want to help." Ashley picked up a couple of the legs.

"Careful." Seth gathered a bunch in his arms. "Come on, Ash, you can hold the door open."

Jake collected the last of the large chunks. "We'll be right back."

"I'll start breakfast." If only it would be as easy to pick up the pieces of her children's lives. "Do you want coffee?"

"No, I think I'll skip it this morning."

She spotted the coffeepot under the table. "Me, too."

# *Chapter Twenty-Two*

Jake soaked the small woodpile with the diesel he found in the barn. He put the can back in the barn and made sure the kids stood at a safe distance before he dropped a match on the ruined table.

Remembering the night of Vickie's personal bonfire, he understood the desire to burn a nasty relic.

"Can you make it bigger?" Seth shouted.

Jake looked up to the sky. The drizzle increased until another full-fledged rainstorm fell on them. "The rain might put it out."

Ashley pulled her jacket over her head. "It's raining. I'm going inside to help Mommy."

After she disappeared around the trailer, Jake moved closer to Seth. "That was a rough scene. How you holding up?"

The kid gave his classic teen shrug. "I'm fine."

"It's okay to be angry, scared or even confused. Speaking from experience, I know it's tough."

Seth shoved his hands into the front pockets

of his hoodie. "What? You want me to cry like a baby?"

"No, I want you to feel safe talking about it and know you did the best you could. It's okay to cry if you want to." Jake hoped he could give Seth what he didn't even know he had needed twenty years ago. "Your father made the mistake. You stepped up and stopped him. You're a hero."

"No, I…was so afraid." His voice broke. "He tossed her like she was a piece of trash. I just stood there. I was…"

Jake shoved down his own emotions and nodded. "You felt helpless."

"Yeah, but then I saw the gun sitting on the counter. I know I'm not supposed to mess with guns. Papa Jack has taken me to the safety courses and range. I thought if I could just point the gun at him, he'd stop."

Jake could guess what happened then. Once enraged, Tommy wasn't going to let anything get in his way. He knew Seth had to talk about it, so as not to make it a dark secret that festered and warped every choice he made from here on out. "Did he stop?"

"No." Seth wiped his sleeve across his face. After a moment of silence, he looked up at Jake. "He laughed at me. I thought about you killing your dad. For a minute, it sounded like a real good idea, but then I remembered you saying God had been there but you didn't realize it." He shoved his hands back into the front pockets of his hoodie. "I prayed and asked God what to do. That's when I saw it, his face in our family picture. Like a target at the practice range. I shot it instead of him."

Jake's heart twisted and his eyes burned. Somewhere along the telling of his story, Seth had started crying. Jake pulled him into his arms.

Seth hid his face in the blue material of Jake's shirt. The tough teen turned back to the little boy. "I almost killed my father. Why was he hurting her?"

"He's made some bad choices, but they were his choices. He lost control, but he doesn't have any power over you or the man God means for you to become."

"But he's my father, the only one I have."

"No, he's not. God is your ultimate Father. You have Papa Jack and you have me. Pastor John and Rhody want to help, too. We are all here for you, Seth."

Seth separated himself from Jake and rubbed his face. He looked to the trailer. "I'm glad Ashley didn't see how Dad acted." With a sigh loaded down by problems bigger than his shoulders, he looked at Jake. "Do you think Mom's really okay?"

"Your mother's one of the strongest people I know. As long as you and your sister are safe and happy, she'll be fine."

"Do you like her, like want to date her?"

"Seth, I love your mother, and I hope she'll agree to marry me one day in the future."

Seth's eyes went wide and he stepped back. "She didn't say anything."

"Because I haven't told her yet." Jake shoved his hands in his pockets and glanced at the trailer, hoping he hadn't said the wrong thing. "I wanted to talk to you and get some things in order before I asked." He met Seth eye to eye. "What do you think?"

A big grin destroyed the seriousness of Seth's expression. "Don't you think you should date a little first?" He looked at the fire and shrugged. "She smiles a lot with you around."

"That's good to know. I have loved your mom for a long time. I'll think about the dating thing."

Seth nodded. The gravity reappeared on his face. "What about Dad?"

Jake put his hand on the nape of Seth's neck. "We'll let the law and God take care of him. Any other concerns?"

The rain fell harder. "No, not right now."

"If anything comes up, don't hesitate to call me, anytime. Got it?"

"Yeah."

Jake squinted and looked across the hills that surrounded them. "The clouds are coming in fast. Let's make sure the fire's out and go get some breakfast."

Vickie couldn't stop the tears after seeing Seth in Jake's arms.

"Mommy?" Ashley rushed to Vickie's side. Concern clouded her daughter's eyes.

"I'm fine."

"Where are we going to eat?"

Vickie scanned her small living space. The bar had only two stools. Most of the time the kids used the coffee table, but it was history.

If she pulled the table away from the wall, four could sit there, but her sewing equipment and material covered the surface.

"Help me put all this stuff in my room. We'll eat from the table like a real family."

She picked up the uncut material for Lorrie Ann's dress and gave it to Ashley.

Carrying an arm full of emerald satin, Ashley vanished under the sea of material. "Mommy, Rachel and Celeste are going to look like princesses. I can't wait."

She thought of how Pastor John's girls had lost their mother. There was more than one way to lose a parent. They seemed to really love Lorrie Ann.

With the craft box in hand, Vickie followed Ashley. "I hope so. Be careful."

"Will you make me a princess dress when you marry Officer Torres?"

Vickie froze. "What makes you think I'm going to marry Jake?"

"Mommy! We saw you kissing in the rain and Grandma said we had better start planning a wedding, because it was long overdue." After carefully straightening the material over the bed, Ashley turned back to her mother. "What did she mean?

Papa Jack said his mare was long overdue and then she had a baby. Are y'all going to get married and have a baby? I'd love a sister."

Her seven-year-old daughter stood looking at her like they were having the most natural conversation in the world. "Well…" Vickie swallowed. "I like Jake and I think he likes me. So we will probably date then go from there." She pushed a loose strand of blond hair from the little face. "How do you feel about Jake being part of our life?"

"I like it a lot. I'd like a sister even more." She bit her bottom lip, and studied her mother. "Is that why Daddy got mad? He didn't want you to date someone else?"

Vickie sat on the edge of the bed. "Your dad lost control because he let anger and money take over his life."

Ashley joined her on the bed and laid her head in Vickie's lap. "I don't like that Daddy hurt you."

Vickie refused to cry. Stroking her daughter's hair, she took a breath and prayed for the right words. "Yes, it was wrong. No one has the right to hurt another just to get what they want. As long as your father is a threat to us, he won't be in our lives. We have Papa Jack, Grandma, Officer Torres and so many good people in Clear Water that love us. Most important we have God."

"Are we going to move in with Officer Torres?"

"No, but we will be moving into Grandma's pool house. We should be closer to someone for now."

She felt Ashley nod her head against her lap. She still wore her flowered dress and pink boots. "Do you want to change since we're not going to church today?"

"Should I throw my boots away?"

"Oh, babe, they are just boots. If you like them it's okay." She heard the door open, and for a second her heart made a nosedive to her stomach.

"Vickie?" Jake's deep timbre filled the trailer.

All her muscles relaxed. "We're in the back. Be out in a minute." She studied the delicate features of her baby girl. "You ready for some pancakes?"

"Yes!" Ashley jumped up and ran to the kitchen. Vickie followed.

"I smell bacon!" Seth said with his nose in the air. He was headed straight to the stove about to pick up a strip when Vickie stopped him.

"Wait a minute. We're going eat like a family should, at the table." All she really wanted to do was curl up with her babies and cry, but that wouldn't do anyone any favors. Instead, she chose to smile and push ahead. "Go wash your hands and get the other chair from your room."

"Oh, Mom, just one piece, please?"

Jake laughed as he headed to the sink. "Come on, the sooner we do what she says, the faster we get to eat." He winked at her as he walked to the kitchen.

Removing the last of the items from her workstation, she asked Ashley to wipe off the tabletop. She poured the batter over the hot griddle and started stacking pancakes. She had Seth add the syrup and orange juice to the table along with the bacon. She pretended not to see him sneak a piece. "Ashley, go ahead and bring the silverware and glasses. Seth, get four plates out."

"Wow, we usually just get paper plates."

"This is fun, Mommy." Ashley scooted into the smallest space between the back wall and table. This would be their last meal in this house.

She looked across the stack of pancakes and found Jake staring at her. She dropped her gaze, uncomfortable, knowing she looked a mess. Glancing back up, she found him smiling.

"Jake, will you say grace?" she asked.

He nodded then held out his hands for Ashley and Seth. She did the same, creating a family circle. She put her head down and breathed through her nose. She would not cry.

# Chapter Twenty-Three

The worst day in her life happened over a week ago, and she was sure life would never be the same again. Her biggest worry was Seth. She thanked God for Jake and Pastor John's mentor program. If not for that, she might have lost her son. Jake had helped move her basic essentials into her parents' pool house. The little bungalow was smaller than the trailer, and the kids had to share a room. She thought they would put up a fuss, but it seemed most nights they all ended up in her bed, anyway. After the nightly Bible story and prayer, she just didn't have the heart to send them away.

That had been one week ago. Stirring the ground beef, she breathed in the aromas that drifted throughout their new living space. She glanced over at her vibrating phone. Lorrie Ann had replied to her text, setting up a time to get her measurements.

Seth ran into the living area. "Is dinner ready?"

"Almost." She smiled at him. "Set the table, please."

"Yes, ma'am."

Vickie hummed as she starting cutting tomatoes. Two days ago, her mother helped her create a sewing center in one of the guest rooms at the big house. It rubbed a little raw that she had to use her parents' house, but she reminded herself that was just pride talking. She definitely had more room for the projects in that one room than she did in the trailer.

As soon as she started on Lorrie Ann's wedding gown the extra room would be appreciated. The rest of the dresses for Pastor John and Lorrie Ann's wedding hung in the walk-in closet, ready for their last alterations.

Yes, the space was good because in the past week, she had picked up more jobs, some custom drapes and prom dresses. Along with her hours at the store, she didn't have much time to think of anything else. Busy was good.

Her kids kept her focused at night.

A part of her wished she had taken Jake up on his offer. Living in the cottage on his place would have put them closer and offered her more independence, but he hadn't mentioned it again and she hadn't asked. Maybe he had just suggested it out of kindness. Jake was the kind of guy who always did the right thing. She imagined how it would be to see him every day.

Last Sunday when she saw him at church, they

talked for just a moment before Lorrie Ann had taken her away to talk about the dresses. She smiled, remembering him sliding into the pew next to her and the kids. He wore his uniform. He must have left straight to patrol because he had gone before they finished the last hymn.

"Mom, what are you doing?" Seth's impatient voice cut through her thoughts.

With a start, she refocused on grating the cheese. Her mother had invited Jake over for dinner and he had turned her down, claiming to have to work. Nevertheless, he hadn't asked her out on a date yet. Of course, neither had she. Maybe the mess with Tommy ended up being too much for him.

Vickie feared they had fallen into their old patterns of not talking to each other. She sighed, fighting the sadness that tried to settle in her heart. She needed to count her blessings, instead.

"Ouch." She cut her knuckles before realizing the block of cheese was gone. She checked the bowl of cheddar to make sure it was clean as she sucked on her finger. She ran her hand under the water. Seth grabbed the last bowl and put it on the table before looking at her with expectations.

She nodded. "Get your sister."

"Ashley, dinner's ready!" Seth called out.

"Really, Seth? I could have done that."

He grinned and slid into his chair. Since the breakfast after Tommy's attack, she had made sure they ate their meals together at the table.

Seth started piling up his plate. Here lately, he ate twice as much as she and Ashley combined.

Good thing she worked at the Mercantile.

"Tacos! Thank you, Mommy." Ashley climbed into the chair on Vickie's right.

"Seth, would you say grace, please?"

"Yes, ma'am." He bowed his head and took Ashley's and Vickie's hands in his.

Vickie swallowed a lump in her throat. He had learned that from Jake. "Dear Lord, thank You for our family and friends. Please keep everyone safe. Thank You for a safe place to live and the food on the table. Amen."

Pride swelled in her heart. She sent him a smile before turning her attention to Ashley. Helping her daughter add cheese and lettuce to her taco, she thanked God for these small moments. "So how was your day, Seth?"

Mouth full of rice, he answered her. "I finally beat Rachel on a math test. I got a 98, she only got a 95." He was about to take another bite of his taco but stopped. "Oh, Mom, I forgot to tell you. Last night at youth group, Jake gave me a message for you." He took the bite and started chewing.

She raised her eyebrows and tilted her head. Really? He was going to leave her hanging after dropping that? "Seth?"

Ashley wiggled in her chair, bouncing up and down. "He wants us to come over for a bonfire! We get to make s'mores."

"I was supposed to tell her," Seth grumbled as he glared at his little sister.

She stuck her tongue out at him then giggled. "You had food in your mouth."

"Guys, it doesn't matter who tells me. Is that all? When does he want us to come over?"

"Friday. With all the rain we've had lately, he said we can build a big fire." He attacked another taco.

Maybe this was it, just the four of them. She thought of the night he found her at the bonfire, burning her wedding pictures.

She smiled at the memory of him putting out the fire and lecturing her about the dangers of open flames. She sighed while the kids kept talking about how big Jake could build a fire and made her own taco.

How romantic. Excitement and anticipation jumbled her heart. She glanced at the devotional calendar on the wall, only four days until Friday. She'd take him some of the cookies his mother had refused to make for him.

# Chapter Twenty-Four

Dumbfounded, Vickie sat in her car. The engine idled as she stared at Jake's two-story cabin. She couldn't believe it. Several vehicles filled his driveway, including Pastor John's truck, her parents' car and the Buchannans' SUV, along with a few other cars she didn't recognize.

She watched as Maria greeted the Levi family on the front porch. They smiled and laughed. The tiny woman led them through Jake's front door. As it closed, the cut glass caught the last rays of the setting sun, creating a rainbow of colors in its reflection.

"Rachel's here!" Seth jumped out. He stopped at Vickie's door and tapped on the window. "Mom? What are you doing?"

"Oh, sorry. I was lost in thought." Well, so much for a romantic night with Jake. He had invited her to a social.

With a sigh, she cut the engine and grabbed the

cookie platter in the passenger's seat. Smiling at her son, she got out of the car. "Come on, let's go join the party."

Before Vickie's boot hit the top step, Maria opened the front door and welcomed them with a gleam in her eyes.

"Hello, Vickie. Seth, Ashley. Everyone's already around the fire if you want to go out back."

Ashley gave Jake's mother a quick hug before following her brother through the house.

"Welcome, Victoria." Maria stepped back, leaving the door wide open. "Come in, come in." She took the cookies. "Oh, you didn't need to bring anything. Jake's in the kitchen, follow me." The tiny woman turned to the left and started walking without a backward glance.

Vickie paused for a moment. She took one step into Jake's house, a home he built with his own hands. Her hand lingered on the wood frame. A cozy sitting area opened to her right, with custom bookshelves that went to the ceiling.

She slowed her steps and took in Jake's home. His very essence was in every room. Following Maria, Vickie skimmed her fingertips along the cream-colored walls. In the hallway to the kitchen, black frames of different sizes covered the wall. Pictures of Jake filled many of them, him in school, the marines, with his sister and mother.

She stopped. In a small frame she saw her own face, laughing with Jake as they jumped off the

Lawson Bridge. His sister had taken it the summer before they went into high school. The memory, connected to so many emotions, flashed before her eyes as if it had just happened. The day had been blistering hot, and she dared him to jump. At first he had told her no, but like so many times before, he joined her. He wouldn't let her go alone. Her finger fluttered over their young faces.

She smiled. A neighbor had been driving by and before she got home, her mother had already heard about the stunt. Of course, Elizabeth had blamed it all on Jake. Her smile went deeper. She'd been grounded for three weeks, and it had been worth every minute.

"Vickie?" Maria's voice came from the kitchen area around the corner. "Well, she was right behind me."

"That's okay, *amá*, take these outside. I'll get her."

Vickie heard some mumbling words in Spanish then the door closing.

"Hey." Jake stood at the corner, one shoulder against the wall, his hands in the back pockets of his jeans.

"Hey," she whispered back. The house suddenly seemed unnaturally silent.

Pushing off the wall, he joined her in looking at the wall of photos. "Oh, so this is what caught your attention?"

Her gaze followed the lines of his strong profile.

"Why is this picture of me on your wall with the family photos?"

He shrugged before looking back at her. "That was the best summer of my life. My sister thought it was the best photo she had ever taken. When we were picking the pictures for the wall, it got a two-to-one vote."

She nodded, one side of her mouth pulled up. "I'll take three guesses who voted against it, and the first two won't count."

Jake snorted. "Oh, I'm sure my mother's gotten over that. Let's go to the kitchen." He turned and headed out of the hall. "Speaking of voting, there is something I need to tell you."

With a hesitant step, Vickie followed him. Now would be the best time to talk to him, before people surrounded them. She paused under the archway opening to his kitchen and large family room, anchored with a giant U-shaped leather sofa covered in dark greens and reds. "Oh, Jake, this is beautiful." She looked back at him with a smile.

His gaze roamed around the room, seeming to avoid her. "You like it? The colors could be changed."

"No, it's perfect the way it is." The space between them felt awkward and heavy, filled with undeclared emotions. Maybe it was just her.

"I'm glad you like it." His hands rested on the dark granite island with his head down. "Like I was saying." He cleared his throat and glanced back at her. "I want to talk to you." He moved from the counter to the black refrigerator.

She noticed the artwork on the double doors. Three childish drawings lined up neatly in a row. The first she recognized as the one from Cassie's son, the day at the drugstore. The second one was from Ashley. They were all on horses with the river going through the middle. She didn't know the third one, but she could guess where he got it. It was a big heart with a teddy bear and a police car.

Mustard, ketchup and relish started lining up on the counter as he pulled them out.

She waited. He gave her nothing but silence. Why would he say he wanted to talk but then not say anything? "Jake?"

He cleared his throat again. "Yeah, so knowing how you feel about politics—" He ran his fingers through his thick, dark hair. "—I've decided not to run for sheriff."

Shock robbed her of words for a moment, but only a moment. Moving forward, she used the counter to hold her up. "Being sheriff of Clear Water means everything to you. Why would you do this?"

"Your vote is the only one that counts. Winning the town's support without you would be—" He shrugged. "—I don't know…empty." He leaned across the counter and looked straight into her eyes. "I want to give us a chance, and if that means not running for sheriff, then I'll stay a state trooper."

Her insides turned to jelly. Maybe tonight was more than just another get together with friends and family. Being sheriff would be a dream come true for him.

She couldn't fathom him giving it up. She didn't want him to give it up. Her legs felt weak. Glancing around, she pulled a padded stool out and sat.

Vickie set her red bag in front of her and dug around until she found the little poster she had folded up into quarters.

"Jake, you need to fulfill God's purpose in your life. If that means you become sheriff, then that's what you do." She unfolded the paper. "I can't be the reason you quit before you even start." Vickie held it up for him to read. *Jake Torres, a man you can trust, at all times.* "It needs a little work but with my cheerleading and committee background, I think I can make a good campaign manager."

Looking at her handwritten sign, Jake took the paper from her. With a sweet half smile, he laid it between them. "Vickie, I know you hated campaigning when Tommy ran for the Senate." He reached over the sign and took her hand. "I want you in my life more than I want to be sheriff. Anyway, I have to resign from the DPS before I can make it official." Releasing her hand, he took a step back. "I haven't done that yet."

"If we want to have a future together we can't assume to know what the other wants. I want you in my life, and I want to support you for sheriff."

She looked down at her hands and pulled on her fingers, not sure what to do with her hands now that he had let them go. "But I have to clear up the loose ends with Tommy." Raising her gaze, she looked at Jake. "I don't want you to come in and save me."

"What's wrong with me saving you?" His voice came from a gritted jaw. He looked over his shoulder, out the window. "You could be there for me and I get to be there for you." Bringing his face back around, he looked directly into her eyes. "Do you trust God to be strong enough take care of our future?"

She wanted to say yes so badly it hurt, but she had other worries. How could she explain herself without it sounding like rejection or a lack of faith?

She sighed. "Yes, but it's not about you and me at the moment, Jake. I have Seth and Ashley to take care of. I have to make sure they're going to be okay. After everything with Tommy, I worry about them, especially Seth." She folded the corners of the paper sign. She had hoped her support for his run would have made him happier. He almost seemed upset.

"Vickie, I understand. Especially after everything you've learned about me."

She moved to the other side of the granite slab, covering his hand with hers. Cotton balls took up residence in her throat. When she finally got a word out, it sounded hoarse and raw, even to her own ears. "Jake." Moving her fingers up, she caressed his clean-shaven face. Sliding her hand down, she cupped his jaw. "Even at your worst you're still the best man I know." She had fallen in love with this man when she was only nine years old. Now her heart swelled with even more love than she thought possible.

"This is not about your father. If Seth grows into at least half of the man you are, I would be so proud. I'm proud to know you."

Jake's mouth opened, but before he could get any words out the back door banged against the wall. Seth and Rachel rushed into the kitchen.

"Mom, we've been waiting for y'all. Papa Jack said the ribs and hot dogs are done and we need the ketchup."

"Relish and mustard, too." Rachel added.

Seth turned up his nose. "Mustard, gross."

Rachel hit him on the shoulder. "You can't have hot dogs without mustard."

Seth shrugged and smiled at her. "I'll try the mustard, if you add ketchup to your dog."

Rachel made a face at Seth before grabbing the bottles and heading for the door.

"We were told to get the chili, too." Seth looked at his mom. "Are you coming outside?"

Jake moved to the opposite side of the kitchen. "I'll get the chili. Vickie, get a spoon out of that drawer there." With black mittens, Jake took the pot of chili off the stove. "Come on. Seems the party started without us."

Walking to the large, farm-style sink, Vickie took a moment to look past the detailed woodwork to the backyard. She studied the world Jake had created in his own little valley.

Her gaze traveled from the Victorian cottage to stables and barns and the gazebo with the stone… Wait. What in the world? Surprise locked her in place. Narrowing her eyes, she stared at the group of people sitting and standing around the limestone fire pit.

Yes, she had seen what she thought she had seen. Her two sisters, Annie and Di sat with Esmi, his sister. "I thought your sister was in Boston." She turned back to him. "My sisters are out there, too. When did they get into town? What's going on?"

Glancing back through the window, she saw the Buchannans with their four boys standing next to Pastor John, Lorrie Ann and Yolanda. Her parents sat with Maria.

"Surprise!" Jake gave her a lopsided grin from the doorway.

"Surprise, for what?" This was for her? Hands on hips, she raised her eyebrows.

Looking to the ceiling, Jake scanned the room before responding. "Happy birthday?"

"My birthday is next month, Jake Torres."

He smiled. The smile that melted her heart. "If we had waited until next month it wouldn't have been a surprise."

She rolled her eyes. "This is not for my birthday."

"Everyone is having fun without us, and they are demanding the chili. Stop worrying and enjoy the evening. Okay?"

He nudged the door open. The laughter and music drifted up the stone pathway into the kitchen. With spoon in hand, Vickie slipped past Jake and headed to the gathering.

The last rays of sun fought to hold ground behind the western hills, giving up to the night. Vickie looked to the sky, following the wisps of flames as yellow and orange curled and danced toward the stars.

For a moment, she focused on the silhouetted hills surrounding Jake's backyard. The fresh smell of rain in the trees mixed with leather and bonfire. Comfort and peace settled around her.

"Vickie!" Arms surrounded her in a big hug. Both of her sisters and Esmi had her in an embrace.

"Annie, Di, what are y'all doing here? Esmi, it's so good to see you."

"Oh, we wouldn't miss tonight for anything." Everyone smiled at her.

"But why are…"

"Here's the chili!" Jake interrupted her. "Y'all can catch up later. I think everyone is ready to eat." His announcement brought cheers from the kids.

Vickie allowed herself to absorb the perfect moment of all her family and friends. A spirit of gratitude wrapped around her heart. This place, this valley, felt like home. Maybe she should have rented the cottage from Jake, after all.

Vickie looked at Jake. She had loved him from the first moment he had walked into her life. He understood her in a way no one else ever had, including her parents.

He moved to stand in front of her. She gasped as Jake dropped to one knee in front of her, in front of everyone.

Complete silence fell over the party. Even the horses watched from their stalls. Jake coughed. "When we were in sixth grade, you asked me a question."

His lips pulled to the side and the dimple she loved so much dug deeper into his cheek. He pulled a red, paper heart out of his jacket and lifted it to her.

Her hands flew to her mouth. In his hands was the Valentine's Day card she had made for him in fifth grade? That day he laughed at her.

"Victoria Maria Lawson, if your offer still stands—" he looked down briefly before turning his dark eyes back to her "—my answer is yes."

He opened the card and inside was a diamond ring.

"Jake?" she whispered, afraid this was one of her dreams. What if it wasn't real? She stared at him; not a word managed to find its way from her brain to her mouth.

His smile faltered. "I'm trying to be romantic, but apparently, I dragged out the suspense a little too long. Sorry." His rich, brown eyes looked tortured.

He slipped the ring from the card and held it up to her. The stone sparkled in the firelight. He stayed on his knees, holding the ring up to her.

Tears gathered in her eyes.

He dropped his hands, the beautiful ring disappearing in his fist. "Vickie, I fell in love with you from the minute I saw you bottle-feeding orphaned lambs."

His throat worked up and down. "I love you more today than I ever thought possible. I can't imagine not having you in my future. Together, we can figure everything else out. I promise to stand by you forever. No running."

She just stood there, frozen, staring down at him. Years of impossible dreams coming true clogged her brain.

His knees popped as he straightened. Standing, he pulled her into his arms as if he understood how overwhelming the actual moment was for her. Without his strength, she might have fallen over.

His voice caressed her ear. "Victoria Maria Lawson, will you marry me?"

She managed to nod against his chest. She didn't

want to let go of this moment. Her family, the fire, the stars and Jake's love all coming together in one perfect place.

He drew away from her. "Can I put it on your finger?"

She nodded again and looked at the ring. Bands of gold swept around the diamond. It reminded her of her favorite painting, Starry Night.

"I know it's not big, but when I saw…"

"It's absolutely perfect." She watched his strong, callused fingers gently slip the ring over her knuckle. It was really happening. She was going to be his wife. For a moment, her lungs quit working.

"Um, Seth, now would be a good time."

"Oh, sorry." With a click, the song she had picked for their prom dance that never happened started playing.

Vickie wanted to stare at Jake all night. Whenever she looked at him before, she had seen her first love, now she saw her future. Peace settled around her heart. "Thank you."

His gaze met hers, the dark lashes surrounding the most amazing eyes she had ever seen.

Leaning in, he whispered against her cheek. "May I have this dance?"

She couldn't stop grinning as she placed her hand in his. Bliss and laughter bubbled up inside her.

Jake guided her away from the fire toward the open patio, and they danced with the people she loved watching.

As Jake's arm went around her waist, family and friends faded into the background.

With the stars overhead, and white lights strung through the tree branches, their song played again. Her heart sang along as he whispered the words into her ear. Their steps floated on joy and love as Jake spun them toward the future God had intended all along.

\* \* \* \* \*

Dear Reader,

I'm excited to have the opportunity to share Vickie and Jake's story. Vickie has been a bit difficult to write. When she appeared in the first Clear Water story, I had no intention of her being the next heroine, but Jake said something that made me start thinking about why she was the way she was— why do women say mean things about each other? Once I dug deeper, I knew I had to write her story. She needed to trust God completely with her whole life and be open to his plan and so did Jake. They both made some choices that they regretted and had some growing up to do before they could get to their happy ending. Hope you enjoy their journey.

I would like to thank the brave law-enforcement officers that answered my many questions, especially Lester Beaver for taking out time from the football game. Any errors are completely mine.

I do have to confess that the opening scene is very real. Yes, you can forget about a ticket and end up with a warrant and the officer can be very helpful. That is the great thing about being a writer— you find yourself thinking, *Hey, I could use this in my story.*

Clear Water, Texas, is in many ways home to me. Even though the name is fictional, parts of it are very real. If you want to see some of the inspiration for the town and people, please check out my Pinterest boards at www.pinterest.com/jolenenavarro.

You can find out more about me on my site, jolenenavarrowriter.com. I also love to visit on Facebook: www.facebook.com/jolenenavarrowriter. I would love to hear from you.

*Jolene Navarro*

## Questions for Discussion

1. Which character of Clear Water, Texas, stands out to you? Why?

2. Do you have a favorite scene? What makes it work for you?

3. In the beginning of the book, Vickie is burning pictures of her wedding day. Do you think she is overreacting or just healing from broken dreams? How do you get past old hurts?

4. Vickie has the reputation of being the "mean girl" from high school. When she moved back, divorced and bitter, she fell into that role again. Do you think people can change and did you believe Vickie's change of heart? What made that change real?

5. Jake knows he is still struggling with old feelings for Vickie. Why do you think he has never told her how he feels? Do you ever ignore issues because they are too difficult to deal with or do you know someone else that does this? How can God help us with this?

6. Because of the divorce, Vickie's relationship

with her son is strained. Do you think she could have handled it in a different way? How does divorce affect children? Are there things parents can do to make it easier?

7. Jake and his mother had a secret that they held on to for many years. Do you think that secret shaped their futures even if they didn't talk about it? Why or why not?

8. As a teenager, Jake ran when life got complicated. As an adult he still struggled with real emotion and conflict. Why do you think that is?

9. When Tommy returns, trying to win Vickie back, she has hard choices to make. Did she do the right thing by letting him back into the kids' lives, while not letting him back into a relationship with her? Discuss.

10. Jake's mother believed she knew what was best for her son. Instead of going against his mother, he leaves for the Marines. Do you think children need to leave home in order to become their own person?

11. Vickie's mother believed she knew what was best for her daughter. How did this shape Vickie's character?

12. Vickie had said horrible things to Lorrie Ann in the past. Were you able to understand and empathize with Vickie in her attempt to change? Do you think Lorrie Ann did the right thing by not only forgiving her, but asking for Vickie's help?

13. Tommy, Jake and Vickie all had secrets. Do you think there is ever a secret that should stay a secret or do they all need to be told?

14. Elizabeth and Maria wanted to control their children's lives. Trusting God with your children can be difficult. Did you ever have to accept someone in your child's life that you believed was wrong for them? How did you handle it?

15. Vickie struggled with knowing her purpose in life. How do you seek God's purpose in your life? Have you always known it or has it been a journey? Maybe you are still on that journey? Share.

# LARGER-PRINT BOOKS!

## GET 2 FREE
## LARGER-PRINT NOVELS
## PLUS 2 FREE
## MYSTERY GIFTS

*Love Inspired®*
# SUSPENSE
### RIVETING INSPIRATIONAL ROMANCE

### *Larger-print novels are now available...*

**YES!** Please send me 2 FREE LARGER-PRINT Love Inspired® Suspense novels and my 2 FREE mystery gifts (gifts are worth about $10). After receiving them, if I don't wish to receive any more books, I can return the shipping statement marked "cancel." If I don't cancel, I will receive 4 brand-new novels every month and be billed just $5.24 per book in the U.S. or $5.74 per book in Canada. That's a savings of at least 23% off the cover price. It's quite a bargain! Shipping and handling is just 50¢ per book in the U.S. and 75¢ per book in Canada.* I understand that accepting the 2 free books and gifts places me under no obligation to buy anything. I can always return a shipment and cancel at any time. Even if I never buy another book, the two free books and gifts are mine to keep forever.

110/310 IDN F5CC

| Name | (PLEASE PRINT) | |
|---|---|---|

| Address | | Apt. # |
|---|---|---|

| City | State/Prov. | Zip/Postal Code |
|---|---|---|

Signature (if under 18, a parent or guardian must sign)

## Mail to the Harlequin® Reader Service:
### IN U.S.A.: P.O. Box 1867, Buffalo, NY 14240-1867
### IN CANADA: P.O. Box 609, Fort Erie, Ontario L2A 5X3

**Are you a current subscriber to Love Inspired Suspense books
and want to receive the larger-print edition?
Call 1-800-873-8635 or visit www.ReaderService.com.**

* Terms and prices subject to change without notice. Prices do not include applicable taxes. Sales tax applicable in N.Y. Canadian residents will be charged applicable taxes. Offer not valid in Quebec. This offer is limited to one order per household. Not valid for current subscribers to Love Inspired Suspense larger-print books. All orders subject to credit approval. Credit or debit balances in a customer's account(s) may be offset by any other outstanding balance owed by or to the customer. Please allow 4 to 6 weeks for delivery. Offer available while quantities last.

**Your Privacy**—The Harlequin® Reader Service is committed to protecting your privacy. Our Privacy Policy is available online at www.ReaderService.com or upon request from the Harlequin Reader Service.

We make a portion of our mailing list available to reputable third parties that offer products we believe may interest you. If you prefer that we not exchange your name with third parties, or if you wish to clarify or modify your communication preferences, please visit us at www.ReaderService.com/consumerschoice or write to us at Harlequin Reader Service Preference Service, P.O. Box 9062, Buffalo, NY 14269. Include your complete name and address.

LISLPDIR13R

# *ReaderService*.com

## Manage your account online!

- Review your order history
- Manage your payments
- Update your address

*We've designed
the Harlequin® Reader Service
website just for you.*

## Enjoy all the features!

- Reader excerpts from any series
- Respond to mailings and
  special monthly offers
- Discover new series available to you
- Browse the Bonus Bucks catalog
- Share your feedback

*Visit us at:*
**ReaderService.com**

RS13